My Devdas

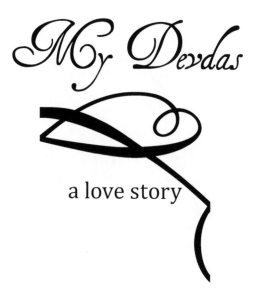

a love story

R. K. Shadid

iUniverse LLC
Bloomington

MY DEVDAS
a love story

iUniverse books may be ordered through booksellers or by contacting:

iUniverse
1663 Liberty Drive
Bloomington, IN 47403
www.iuniverse.com
1-800-Authors (1-800-288-4677)

Because of the dynamic nature of the Internet, any web addresses or links contained in this book may have changed since publication and may no longer be valid. The views expressed in this work are solely those of the author and do not necessarily reflect the views of the publisher, and the publisher hereby disclaims any responsibility for them.

Any people depicted in stock imagery provided by Thinkstock are models, and such images are being used for illustrative purposes only.

Certain stock imagery © Thinkstock.

ISBN: 978-1-4759-8420-0 (sc)
ISBN: 978-1-4759-8422-4 (hc)
ISBN: 978-1-4759-8421-7 (e)

Library of Congress Control Number: 2013905871

Printed in the United States of America

iUniverse rev. date: 6/24/2013

IN THE JOYOUS EVENT THAT THIS WOULD BE MY FIRST AND LAST BOOK, I WOULD LIKE TO DEDICATE IT TO MOST OF THE PEOPLE WHO MADE A DIFFERENCE IN MY LIFE:

-KHALED, HAIFA, TAWFIQ AND FUAD, FOR PUTTING UP WITH ME, AND ACCEPTING ME THE WAY I AM.

-RAED, WITHOUT YOU IN MY LIFE THIS BOOK WOULD NOT HAVE BEEN POSSIBLE.

-TAWFIQ AND MARY, LOVE YOU AND MISS BOTH OF YOU VERY MUCH. I HOPE I CAN MAKE YOU PROUD.

- DAKHLALAH, NAWAL, DIA, MAJDI AND LUBNA, FOR THE ENCOURAGEMENT, YOU TRULY INSPIRE.

- RIZEK, AMAL, LUAY, LANA AND LARA, FOR THE LOVE AND FUN YOU SHARE, ALL MY LOVE AND RESPECT.

-DALAL AND KARIM, WISH YOU DID NOT HAVE TO LEAVE SO SOON, YOU ARE MISSED EVERY DAY.

- SHAHNAZ, HUSSAM, SUZI AND TAMARA, FOR THE UNCONDITIONAL MENTAL AND EMOTIONAL SUPPORT.

-SALIBA, ALWAYS IN OUR HEARTS.

- HALA, SHADI AND MARY, MAY ALL YOUR DREAMS COME TRUE.

- FAWZI, WE MISS YOU.

-SARAH, WOULD HAVE LOVED TO HAVE YOU AROUND MORE.

-AKRAM, FOR ALWAYS BEING THERE FOR THE FAMILY.

-SOMEBODY TOLD ME I SHOULD THANK DONYA AND NOOR, CAN'T WAIT TILL I CAN WRITE YOU A STORY.

THANK YOU ALL, LIFE WOULD NOT HAVE BEEN THE SAME WITHOUT YOU.

A SPECIAL THANK YOU GOES OUT TO ALL THE PEOPLE OUT THERE WHO STILL BELIEVE IN KINDNESS.

AND FINALLY, A THANK YOU TO MY 'DEVDAS'---LIFE IS NOT WORTH LIVING WITHOUT MY DREAMS.

"God grant me the serenity to accept the things I cannot change, the courage to change the things I can, and the wisdom to know the difference."
Reinhold Niebuhr

One
Not my life

California, July 2001

It was no use, no matter how long she stared at the blank screen, nothing seemed to happen! She realized it was not the computer's fault that she was getting nowhere, her mind was wandering all over the place, and she could not concentrate. Maybe if she had a cup of tea, it would help. Danya looked across the hallway with dismay as she heard the loud banging that came from the room Fadi had assigned as his own personal office. *Does he really have to wrestle with his things to organize that room?* She thought to herself. Since they had decided on the wedding date, and that they would live in her house afterwards, Fadi had been bringing more and more of his things over, and moving out more of hers! *Who but mama's precious boy would think of paying so much money to buy that strange gold frame for his diploma, and then to try and hang it up in the family room next to our hideous engagement picture?* She'd had to insist that he move it into his office. Danya turned in the black leather chair to look at what had become of her house. They had been engaged for six months when Fadi and his parents had decided they were ready for them to get married, and to start a family. She had tried to reason with Fadi: "How exactly could anybody prepare for, and organize, a big wedding in only a month? You know I have a deadline to meet by the end of the month. I thought this would be a decision we make together, not you and your mother... who is getting married here, really?"

Fadi had come and put his arm around her shoulders, steering her towards his office. Once inside, he seated her in a chair, and then he sat behind his desk. True, he was an accomplished architect, but he made her feel like she was visiting a shrink when he sat like that, he even used that too-calm tone that people usually use when talking to a disturbed person. "I have no doubt you will be able to pull it off Danya, you always do". And that had been the end of that conversation.

On another occasion, Danya and Fadi were sitting with his parents around the dining table at Fadi's house, and Danya made the 'unforgivable' suggestion that they could have a smaller, more intimate wedding. Rose, Fadi's mother, was beside herself.

"If you're not having a big wedding, why don't you just go to city hall and get it over with? Unless the wedding is grand, I will not show up, and neither will my husband." She then turned to glare at Issa, her husband of thirty years, and the poor man just nodded along. He had learned a long time ago not to bother and argue with Rose. Fadi, of course, agreed to what his mother wanted—it had been hard afterwards for Danya not to resent Fadi and his parents and not to absolutely hate everything about her wedding—well, except maybe the cake! *Chocolate cake has to be one of the secret ingredients in sanity pills!* Danya surmised as she turned her attention to the state of her house. She looked around again, and again it seemed like there was no safe and quiet place in her house anymore, a move to the roof did not sound too bad, except that the sun outside would be a bit too much for her already fried brain.

Fadi's voice cut into her trip down memory lane with persistence. "Danya, are you okay?"

"Hah?" She winced as she came out of her shell to look up into the worried face that towered over her. "I have been talking to you and asking you if you're okay, and you just have this blank look on your face, like you did not really see me."

Danya figured that what actually bothered him was not that she did not respond, but that she did not see 'him'.

"I'm fine, thank you, just thinking about this book."

"Are you sure? You look a bit tired, and out of it."

"Really, I'm fine." She tried to turn around in her seat and get back to work, and away from him, but Fadi persisted. "Come on Danya, out with it. What's going on?"

"I told you, I'm absolutely fine. Please do not worry yourself about me." And she managed to turn her chair away, mumbling: "So you could go back to whatever it is you are doing in that room." Fadi was a very handsome man. He had beautiful wide hazel eyes, perfectly lined lips, proud tilted nose and a wide forehead crowned with curly golden brown hair that complimented his tanned features. He chose his clothes carefully to show off his wide shoulders and slender hips that fit perfectly with his long and muscular body. Danya always used the word 'perfect' around Fadi and when describing his looks, although of late it came out of habit rather than out of affection. She was brought back to reality when he pushed some of her note papers aside and sat on the edge of the desk to face her.

"Okay Danya, tell me what this really is about."

"Nothing Fadi, really, I'm absolutely fine." She was trying to save some papers from falling into the waste basket, and managed a nice leave-me-alone smile before saying through gritted teeth. "It's nothing, I'm just not getting anywhere with my work today, and I can't concentrate. Other than that, I'm fine." And she turned to face the blank screen, hoping against hope that, for once, Fadi would not push her into the corner. Lately she had been feeling like she was living in a trap, so having him nag her into appreciating his presence was not exactly what she would call smart at this point.

"You know it's hard for me, too, to get all of this together on such short notice, but blaming me, and pushing me away is not the answer to your frustrations or mine!" He said with his 'I'm too charming for you to be too mad at me' smile on his face.

"Well Fadi, this was not exactly my idea. If my memory is not playing games with me, you are the one who admired your parents' idea so much, and yet......" She let the words fade. She had to stop herself before she snapped, which was something that she was dreading would happen any day now. It was no use trying to explain to Fadi or convince him for that matter, that he and his mother could not possibly be right all the time. *Not even half the time!*

His finger under her chin turned her eyes to face his and she was breathless for a moment by the beauty of the golden brown glow in his eyes, sometimes it could almost make her forget everything else she knew about their relationship. She was always wary of Fadi lately when he was being too nice to her out of the blue. He had a nasty habit of being real nice to her for a while, only to turn mean and judgmental all of a sudden.

He stroked her chin with his thumb and said gently, "I know we have been working very hard lately, and spending less time together, but I do miss you a lot."

That hit the spot. Leaning into the safety of his arms, resting her head on his chest, breathing in his cologne and feeling his warmth, Danya let out a deep sigh. She could not but admit that this was her life-long dream, to find the love and safety with somebody of her own. Having been an orphan for so long, with no relatives to speak of, she craved the feeling of belonging. She was feeling very content for a moment—and then Fadi spoke.

"You know I wanted to get married soon, so we could start our life together, move in together and actually be able to go on a real trip together, which we could not do before, and can't even do now even though we're engaged. My parents had nothing to do with this decision. I'm sorry you are getting so stressed over the wedding and the book." He stroked her hair back from her forehead and planted a kiss there. "Maybe you should just hire somebody to help you out a bit, a wedding planner or even a secretary."

"I'll be fine—I'll manage." Danya tried to close her eyes and relax, just to enjoy that moment, but amazingly her Mr. gorgeous had to keep on talking to make his point. One more thing she did not admire much about Fadi is he either would ignore her completely and say nothing for hours and even days, or he never knows when to just stop and back off.

"I see you're not getting on well with your book either. If that's bothering you then I think you should just try your hand in pottery."

She backed out of her shelter to look at him, hoping that she misheard him, or at least just misunderstood... "pottery!" She wondered calmly.

"Well, yeah, you know..."

"No actually I don't know." She said stiffly.

The air between them getting colder by the second as Danya sat back in her chair and crossed her arms over her chest, hoping to get some warmth, but it felt as if the cold was from within.

"Well, what I'm trying to say is, since you love art so much, and your book is not going well, maybe you should try something else, like pottery for a change. You used to paint before you started writing, so... I don't know!"

Fadi was mumbling now, and she was getting hotter in the face. *Breathe...breathe...and do not snap!* She kept telling herself. True, Fadi never read any of her four already published books and never seemed to appreciate the fact that she had a really good deal in the works, but still! She had a bit of hope that maybe; just maybe, her utterly confused mind was playing games with her at that moment.

"What exactly are you getting at here Fadi?"

He squared his shoulders defensively, bringing to mind the image of a six year old who knows he's wrong but will not back down... except that a six year old might have been kind of cute instead of infuriating.

"All I'm saying is that you need a more relaxing hobby."

"Hobby", she muttered in disbelief... and then, "HOBBY???" She yelled as she jumped out of her chair, and stormed out of the house in less than one minute. "I could live with the non-appreciation, but this!!" She was talking loudly to herself as she walked, more like stomped. She was seeing black bubbles floating in front of her face as she walked down the street and shoved her way inside the nice and quiet coffee house around the corner from her house. It had been an Italian restaurant once, but was sold about five months ago to a new owner who obviously spared no expense in remodeling the place. It was beautiful and elegant, and the aroma of fresh coffee and herbal tea gave her a happy jolt.

Danya looked around and saw that it was already getting busy for lunch, so she made her way to the smallest table in the corner and sat with her back to the huge mirror mounted on the wall.

What irony, here I was thinking Fadi was the one trying to corner me, so what do I do? I come here and put myself in the corner! Very smart. Danya smiled, shaking her head, and looked at the menu, the name in gold letters on the top informed her that the new name was "Mike's Mochaccino". She looked up at the young woman who came up to her table, whose black and white uniform was definitely nicer than the faded blue jeans and wrinkled white blouse she was herself wearing. But then again, everything about Zaara was stunning: glowing black hair, sparkling dark brown eyes, beautiful features, and tall slim body.

"Hello Danya. How are you?"

Danya smiled into Zaara's face. *Who could resist kindness?* "Pretty good Zaara. How are you feeling now?" She asked her friend. "I'm sorry I did not get a chance to call and check on you today."

"Don't worry about it. I know how your days are. I'm

good, thank you, much better than yesterday. I finally got over my cold and happy to be back at work. Do you want me to get you something to drink? Laura will be here in a minute to take your order, she's getting another table's food out right now."

"No problem, can I have my usual, please?"

As Zaara went to get Danya's order of Earl Gray tea, Danya thought of the first time she met Zaara. Since she had an obsession with India and anything and anyone Indian since childhood she was beyond overjoyed to meet Zaara, to the point that Fadi kept telling her to calm down before she scared the new manager into kicking them out of the restaurant. That was the last time Fadi had accompanied her there. Fadi had zero tolerance for any of Danya's interests that did not concern him personally.

Laura came and after they exchanged the normal pleasantries, Danya ordered the Greek salad, and then Zaara came back with the tea, set it down, and leaned against the chair facing Danya. She was holding a folder in her hand, and she set it on the edge of the table as she asked Danya, "How is your latest book coming along? When did Blake say it was going into print? I just finished 'Not my life' last night, beautiful work."

"Thank you. I have been trying to work on part two, and get the last details for my *lovely* wedding put together, but I have a feeling everything is just not fitting into place right now. My life seems to be moving too fast for me to catch up, you know what I mean?"

"Oh trust me, lately that is all I've been feeling. Listen, I'm going to let you eat in peace, and I will get back to work, but you have to promise to have a cup of coffee with me before you leave."

"You know I would love to."

Zaara grabbed her folder and turned, passing Laura who had just come with Danya's salad. As Zaara went back to the front desk to attend to her manager duties, Danya noticed a small leather picture holder on the floor—she picked it up, and was about to call Zaara when she saw the face that peeked at her through the clear cover of the wallet-size holder. Handsome and perfect were the words she always used to describe Fadi's perfection, but this face. *My God...he is gorgeous!* It was the face of an exceptionally good looking man, in his thirties, with shiny straight black hair that shone even in the photograph, surrounding a long face with high cheekbones, beautiful almond shaped brown eyes that gleamed with the smile that parted his stunningly sensual full lips to show his nicely shaped white teeth. And even though his nose was larger than average, and a bit crooked, it only served to give his face some interesting wild character. *Okay, there's nothing wrong with noticing details... I am a writer!* She told herself as she put the picture aside before Zaara came back her way and saw her already strange friend acting even weirder than usual.

As Danya worked on her salad and stole glances at the photo, she realized that even though she'd known Zaara for almost four months, and they went out for coffee two to three times a week, she really knew nothing personal about her except that she was from India, and that she came to California to study. Danya was mostly interested in knowing all about Delhi, where Zaara was from, since it was one of the many places she dreamt about seeing in India one day. Fadi was not as interested in going to India as going to France or some other European country that Danya had no interest in visiting, but then again, their list of differences was growing by the second nothing was surprising her anymore. If she was to be honest with herself, it was partially her fault, too. She expected too much, and yet at the same time she figured since she had known Fadi for almost six years he should by now have understood her more, or at least tried to since he asked her to marry him seven months ago.

When the place quieted down, Zaara came back, and sat in the chair facing Danya, placing two cups of coffee on the table. "I'm always happy when we have busy lunches, and happier when it's over and things have gone smoothly. This morning the coffee machine and the grill were not working, so it was a bit straining. How did your morning go?"

"As usual, I tried to put some words into sentences, but let's just say that talking to Fadi and having him around me too much do not encourage any bright ideas in my head at all, aside from imagining ways to block his voice and face out of my head long enough to focus—or even better, coming up with ways to cause him some serious physical pain. Scary, I'm telling you!"

Chuckling, Zaara commented: "Maybe you should write about all the political and religious points of view you're always telling me about, you know, change your path from romance for a while. That might make you happier, or at least it might make it easier for you than making a whole story up right now, until you are more settled in your personal life. I mean, these are your personal thoughts so it's something that you don't have to try and come up with, it's already there. Maybe that's what you need, a little bit of a change, to try your hand in something different."

"But I love writing romance. I would like everybody on this planet to have their own 'Happily ever after'."

"I know you do, you are a hopeless romantic, and I keep telling you that. I already lost count of how many times I've said it, and I believe it more every time we sit down and talk."

Danya laughed lightheartedly and asked. "What time do you get off work today?"

"I have another hour. Would you like to do something later on in the evening?" Zaara wondered as she added more sugar to her coffee. That's why she normally preferred Indian chai, it had milk and sugar mixed into it perfectly.

"I was thinking we can have dinner at my house and go rent that new Hindi movie?"

"It wouldn't happen to be another romantic comedy by any chance?"

"Of course, they are the best." Danya said with her most serious tone that could fool no one.

Zaara laughed and took a sip of her coffee, "I told you, hopeless."

Danya then remembered the photo, and handed it to Zaara, who looked a bit shocked at first and then exclaimed, "Oh! You found Devdas!"

Danya said a little breathlessly, "Devdas!" She then looked again at the upside down face of the smiling man, and she actually blushed.

"Yeah, that's Dev. Didn't I ever tell you about him?"

"No, but you better do that today when you come over. I want details." And she got out of her seat, adding, "I have to run now though, I have to go back to what's left of my house, and make sure that Fadi does not throw away my clothes next to make room for more of his things."

Laughing lightly, Danya paid her bill and left. It was a warm day, but she was still feeling cold in her heart, she had to hug herself to keep from shivering.

What a day! She kept thinking as she walked home.

Two
Devdas

To her relief, when Danya got home, Fadi was not there. After she checked around the kitchen for more damages to her belongings, yes, even the kitchen was not safe, she saw the note on the counter. 'Danya, I'm going out to dinner with my parents, and will spend the night in San Jose. Call me when you get in.' Since Danya did not trust herself not to yell at him yet, she crumbled the paper, threw it in the waste basket, and went back into her office, which was actually one of the three rooms, and she turned it into her writing space. When she bought the house she made sure she got something with a lot of windows and enough space for her junk.

She was used to living alone, her parents had passed away in a car accident six years ago, and since then she had been on her own. Sure, Fadi was around a lot, but her relationship with him was more out of need for companionship and a habit of having him around than out of love. It seemed that had become the norm for her: not to do anything out of love anymore. They had met when they both had just started college, and started hanging out and dating as any other Arabic couple would, but instead of growing closer with the years, they were growing farther and farther apart. Whether it was different Personalities or different interests, it seemed that everything was pulling them away from each other, but they held on to the relationship just because. For Danya it was not the fear of being alone that kept her hoping for a better future with Fadi, she was still young and pretty decent looking, but it was the fear of having wasted so many years and having to start over... and yet lately the little things that make or break a marriage were clearly showing to be lacking in their future life together. The more time they spent around each other the more they disliked each other, or at least that's how she was feeling at the moment. "You won't believe how resentful I'm feeling towards him nowadays." Danya was telling Zaara as she set the tea tray on the table. The aroma made Zaara smile.

"Is it chai masala?" It was a statement more than a question. Danya smiled proudly.

"Of course it is. I make it perfectly now, but Fadi hates it, so I have to make two pots of tea whenever he comes over to my house, bringing more of his things." She tried not to sound resentful, but failed miserably.

Zaara smiled and said kindly, "Have you considered that maybe you push his buttons with your obsession with India? I am Indian, and I do appreciate your admiration of my country to the point of it becoming an obsession, but maybe he just does not get it, and it possibly makes him act out."

"What, he's a five year old acting out now! Fine, I will be fair and honest: yes I am a bit too weird about India and everything Indian, but he knew that about me all along and I feel like he humored me before but after we became more involved, he started acting like it's a new hobby that I acquired and he never knew anything about it. That is one of the many things that aggravate me about Fadi, since he has no real passion about anything besides himself and his family. He understands and appreciates nothing and no one. He keeps falling into this pattern where everything I say or do is wrong... trust me, sometimes I think he's trying to make me out an idiot just so he could look so smart next to me. Does that sound too judgmental and mean for me to say?"

Danya settled herself more comfortably on the seat, tucking her feet under her, and sipped her hot tea, cradling the cup in both hands, still trying to get warm, she was shivering with suppressed anger on the inside and outside.

"Well, yes it does make you a bit judgmental, but not mean. Then again, I have met Fadi, and I know he is that way also, so you both tend to push each other to the limits. You bring out the worst in each other for one reason or another and the longer you are around each other, the worse it is, if you don't mind me saying this to you."

"You know I don't mind one bit. I need someone to be honest and tell me things as they truly are. I am very bad tempered these days, and like you said, I tend to see his faults much more clearly than my own. What do you think I should do?"

15

"I think you two need to sit down and have an honest out in the open talk about everything, soon it will be too late to back out if you are not sure of this."

"You are right, as usual... I will try and somehow pry him away from his mother when I attempt talking to him, trust me the woman is all about herself. Did I tell you what happened last week when we went to their house for dinner?"

"Not that I recall, what happened?" Zaara asked as she also made herself more comfortable, drinking the aromatic tea, and enjoying it, Danya really got the making of Chai down perfectly.

Danya was now telling her about the latest showdown between her and the 'mother-in-law from hell' as she referred to Rose sometimes. She was having another fruitless argument with Fadi that day over the degrading way he treats her in front of his parents, who actually thought it was okay of course since the 'poor man' had so much to stress about—and when Danya was attempting to stand up for herself, Rose pretty much jumped at her throat for daring to distress the precious, ill-mannered excuse for a human being that she had for a son.

"The 'horror' of a human being that she is, she's so self-righteous that she thinks she is so much better than everybody else on this planet, and has this holier-than-thou attitude that could send an angel over the edge and give him some good murderous ideas! She's sitting there yelling orders at the pathetic human being that is her husband, and has the nerve to lecture me about how a wife should show respect to her husband! I witnessed that woman shooing away that man as if he was nothing more than a chicken in her way more times than I can count and then she dares to tell me how to act? Yes I have had thoughts of hurting Fadi lately, but I would never ever act on them. How disrespectful would that be to him and even to myself as human beings? The NERVE! And to top it off, Mrs. Drama Queen burst into tears when I tried to correct her misconception about the whole situation and she had a great self-pity fest all by herself... well, with Fadi and his father patting her on the back and looking at me like I was the worst thing that happened to humanity." Danya stopped to catch her breath, and calm her nerves, if self-control was a volcano, hers was bubbling way too close to the surface.

Zaara leaned forward and said kindly, "Such anger could turn to hatred and even self-loathing, Danya. It's very destructive for all who are involved. You really have to think this through and talk to Fadi as soon as you two can sit down by yourselves and figure it all out."

"I know—trust me, I know." Now that she was feeling a tad calmer, Danya refilled both cups, and then turned her attention to her friend once more.

"So, who is Devdas? You never mentioned anything about him before." And she smiled broadly adding, "And don't leave out any details."

They both laughed, and Zaara actually blushed a bit as she said after thinking for a moment.

"Well... Devdas was my first love."

Danya nearly jumped out of her seat. That was for sure a shocking bit of information! Wiping away the tea that spilled on her pants, she asked Zaara about it. "How come you never said anything about him before today?"

"It's because there is nothing to say, notice I said 'was'. We are almost neighbors back in India, we met there of course, and we sort of fell in love with each other as we grew up. Truthfully our parents never hit it off as friends, they were politely formal whenever they all met but never struck a friendship. Dev came here a couple of times after I came to America to finish my studies, but he mainly resides in India. Dev runs his family business as they own one of the biggest tourism companies in India 'Geet'. Anyways, to make a long story short we are from different religious backgrounds and different communities, so our marriage is out of the question, we cannot be together."

"But, why on earth can't you?" It was more of a whisper, and Zaara laughed lightly.

"I just told you why. Dev actually asked his mother. His father is no more. He asked her about three years ago to send a proposal to my parents, and she refused to even discuss the matter with him. I would not even ask my parents, I know the answer, so why bother them and create conflict over nothing."

"How could it be nothing? It's your love and life we are talking about here Zaara."

Danya was leaning forward in her excitement, and Zaara smiled at her eagerness. She answered her patiently. "Danya, you come from the Middle East, you know how hard it is to marry somebody from a different religion, and it's the same in my country. It is about honor, mine as well as my family's, to marry someone from my own community with the same religious beliefs. It makes sense even if it is not always fair, and it makes it easier for everybody involved, including me. For that matter especially me."

Danya sat back deep in thought, when Zaara handed her another surprise. "My marriage has been fixed for the end of august." And she rushed to Danya's side as the latter spluttered her tea, and started coughing. "Are you okay?"

Danya waved her hand in response, got a hold on her breathing, and looked into Zaara's face. "What?" She wondered.

"Yes. His name is Rohan Aryan. I have his picture here if you would like to see it. My parents just told me this morning. I knew there was talk, but I did not want to tell you before I knew for sure that both families agreed on everything."

"Why do you carry Devdas's photo with you if you are convinced that you two are not meant for each other anymore? Don't you think it might be a sign?" Danya argued on stubbornly.

Zaara laughed and said. "Danya, I promise you are like a stubborn child sometimes! I did not realize I still had Dev's photo in my folder until today, it must have fallen when I came to say hello to you earlier today, you have to admit it shows how unorganized I am. Today I was putting all my things in order, and I gave my two weeks' notice at work—it was probably in my locker with the rest of my papers and clothes, and I pulled it out while I was packing my things. You should also know that my parents did not force me to accept this marriage, they put things in motion only after they asked me and they got my approval."

"So, you will be moving back to India!" Danya could not hide the envy in her voice, and Zaara laughed at her.

"Yes. I will miss it here, but I am looking forward to going back home. I miss the colors and the smells the most—I even miss the street vendors with the sweets carts and the noise, all of it really. I have so much packing to do. I don't know where to begin!"

"You know I would love to help. I can come over anytime you need me to, it's not like I'm doing anything during the day aside from daydreaming about what would cause Fadi the worst pain he had ever suffered in his life."

Laughing at Danya's strange, and sometimes wicked sense of humor, Zaara said. "Thank you Danya. I might take you up on your offer sooner than you think."

Danya looked into her friend's face to see if there was any sadness or regrets, but she saw neither. Maybe she was over her love for Devdas—maybe that's how things worked out sometimes. *Whoever said that the first love has to be the last love?*

"What is Rohan like? Have you met him before?" Danya wondered.

"Oh, yeah, we met at family functions and all that, but then I moved here three years ago, and I only saw him twice since then. We do e-mail each other sometimes, so we're not complete strangers, but the marriage thing happened only recently. My parents are overjoyed, they like Rohan and his family very much. I have to say this, his mother is a great woman, and his father is very respectable also, so sorry to rub it in, but looking at the bright side, I will have a wonderful mother-in-law, at least I won't be having a psychopath to live with!"

Danya burst out laughing, and shaking her head at Zaara said. "Oh, sure—enjoy the joke, why don't you?" She then added more seriously. "I still don't get it, I know that's how things work in your country a lot of times and in Jordan sometimes, but it never makes sense to me to marry someone you know nothing about just because your parents think he is a good match. I mean, sometimes you know the person for years, and in the end it turns out you really know nothing about him. Look at me and Fadi, we make a great example."

"Danya, what was the first thing that made you accept Fadi's marriage proposal? He is a Christian, and he's also from Jordan like you. Most of us look for that security in a relationship, whether we realize it or not. I want to get married and start a family, and it makes it so much easier not to have to confuse my children in the future about whose religion they should follow, and even for me, because I am comfortable in my own beliefs and would not change my religion, not even for Dev. I guess that's how I know for sure that I don't love him as much as I once thought I did. Now, let's talk about fun things. You have to come to India for my wedding next month."

Danya's face lit up, and she jumped up and did a little dance. She was finally going: India...Mumbai...Taj Mahal... Goa, all the places she had been reading and obsessing about for so long! *And Devdas!* A small voice whispered in her head. *Really!!*

Zaara was laughing at her, and then took out Rohan's photo. He was a very good looking man indeed, but Danya could only see Devdas' s face dancing in front of her eyes, she actually had to shake her head a couple of times to clear it out and hear what Zaara was telling her. "I will be done working at the coffee house by the end of this week, it turns out they don't need me to stay on for two weeks, so I could help you more with the wedding, we can pack my things, and we can plan for your trip to India, too." Danya sighed contently. All of a sudden she had so much to look forward to.

The next couple of weeks went by fast—lucky for Fadi, because Danya was about ready to dump him he was pushing her to the limits of what was left of her tolerance; for him and all that concerned their wedding. Nothing she did was good enough. Not once did he offer to help with anything, he had no worries aside from how his tuxedo would fit him, and even that he requested that Danya go pick up for him! And yet he managed to complain about every single detail. Zaara was a great help, really, she was a gift sent from heaven, because even though she had her own wedding to worry about, she managed to get everything in order for herself and for Danya in almost no time, the travel plans were coming together for Zaara and for Danya—only. Fadi refused to accompany Danya to India for the wedding. He said he had his work to finish also, so he did not worry himself too much about Danya going alone to India, as for Danya: she was strangely relieved by his choice to stay behind.

"You can go, after you're done with whatever you have to do for your book. Book your flight accordingly. This way when you come back we both could be free to go wherever we want to go, that is if you still want to go anywhere after visiting all those third world countries you're going to."

Danya prayed for patience as she answered. "Of course I'd still want to go somewhere with you Fadi." *Just as long as I don't have to spend too much time with you until then!* And then added, "And really, it's just one country I'm going to. You can hardly call India a third world country, to say so is just insulting to any nation in this world and on this planet. Who on earth decides what country is worth what anyways?"

Not that Fadi ever paid any attention to anything she was saying, he pretty much just nodded his head, waved his hand, and that was the end of one more fruitless conversation.

Zaara called her with great news that same day though,

so it was refreshing to have something else to think about, aside from controlling her temper around Fadi even for the few hours they had to spend together each day.

"Guess what?" Zaara said happily and Danya could tell from her voice that she was excited to the point of breathlessness.

"Tell me. What's going on?"

"I got them—I got our tickets to India. I leave three days before you do. My parents will not hear a word of you staying in a hotel. They almost bit my head off on the phone when I told them I had my friend from 'Amrica' coming home with me, and wanting to stay in a hotel, they have everything ready for us, all we have to do is show up and have a great time, I can't wait to get home."

"Ah! You have no idea how great this all sounds! India with almost two weeks away from everything; and without dealing with Fadi and his tantrums. It is a dream come true."

They both laughed, and Danya added more seriously, "I really don't want to impose on your family though. I mean I'm sure you will have hundreds of family members and friends showing up, your parents will need all the room they have."

"Listen to me carefully, my stubborn, childish and daydreaming friend: we would not have it any other way, and if it makes you feel better, you can stay with me in my room."

"Wonderful...Zaara, you have been the greatest friend ever. I don't know how I could ever re-pay all you've done for me. I'm going to miss you when I don't have you here anymore, I mean, who's going to listen to me whine about my life from now on?"

Zaara laughed happily, and reassured Danya. "You worry about how you will get Jake and Rebu their happily ever after in your book, and let me worry about mine and yours in real life, as for missing me—I'm going to miss you too, so that is your ticket to come to India all the time now."

"As long as I can get Fadi to promise never to join me on trips there, we're set."

Danya was hesitant for a moment, and then she added quickly, "And you are sure, Zaara, that there aren't any regrets concerning Devdas?"

She could hear Zaara sighing, before answering her firmly. "None whatsoever; I know I am doing the right thing or I would not be so happy about my wedding, and I am excited about starting a new life with Rohan. I have never been more positive about anything else in my life."

"I just want you to be absolutely happy and sure."

"I am Danya, I truly am."

But what about Devdas, how does he feel about all of this? Was the thought that kept haunting Danya's mind day and night for reasons she could not understand.

Even though Danya did not have the wedding to worry about as much, since everything was finally falling into place for her and mostly with Zaara's hard work, she still felt unhappy about it, but could not confide it to Zaara. She could not put in words that she felt very abused mentally and emotionally most of the time. Sometimes mental and emotional abuse could be as damaging as physical abuse— sometimes it was even worse. She looked into Fadi's face nowadays to see his love for her there...or even her love for him, but it was just not there anymore, or it was never there to begin with. Maybe it was like Zaara said; Danya and Fadi's relationship was more out of comfort than out of love.

But leaving him did not occur to her— it was not one of her options.

Three
Wedding Bells

In almost no time, it was finally the wedding day, and Danya was putting on the final touches of her make-up, when Zaara called her on her cellular phone, and told her she was running late, she was going to her apartment first to get her dress and then she was going to try and make it to church, if not she was going to meet them at the reception for sure.

"Are you okay Zaara? What happened?"

Zaara did sound like she had a head cold, but she reassured Danya. "Don't worry about me, I'm fine. I am sorry about this mess you're in though. Who can you have stand-in as your maid of honor on such a short notice?" Danya heard the guilt in Zaara's voice and made sure to calm her down, after all she was not hurt, and that's what mattered the most at the moment.

"Don't worry, all of Fadi's cousins wanted in, but I had

said no, so now one of them will have her moment of glory. Are you sure you are okay? Please tell me you did not have a car accident or get hurt?"

"No, no. Nothing that serious happened, really. Please don't worry. I'm fine and I will be there as soon as I get my dress on, I promise."

"Okay...just be careful. Bye."

"Bye. See you in a bit."

Danya hung up the phone, but she was still worried about Zaara, it was not like her to be late, and she did sound sick or like she had been crying on the phone. They had been together at the hairdresser's that morning, and all was well. *Maybe after she went to her apartment she received a distressing call from home?*

Danya called out to Zain, one of Fadi's cousins, and told her what happened, the girl's face split into the widest smile, Danya thought it should be fined. And then she started talking non-stop!

"Oh, I can't wait for my wedding day, you'll see, it's going to be so grand, people will talk about it for the next ten to twenty years. I'm going to have the church filled and decorated with so many flowers people will have to open the windows to be able to breathe."

Danya realized it was Zain's way to comment on the lack of flowers at her own wedding, but she really did not care that much. She was not a big fan of flowers once they were cut, they reminded her too much of funerals, and she'd been to one too many of those. She had stuck to plain and simple with everything, from her simple but elegant dress, to her hair and make-up, to everything that had to do with this miserable occasion that's supposed to be the happiest day of her life.

As she was finishing her last touches, and making small talk with Zain, Fadi came into the room where she was waiting to be escorted by his uncle. She was shocked, mainly because she did believe that it is bad luck for the groom to see the bride before the wedding, and seriously did they need any more bad luck in that relationship! And because Fadi had a look of rage that was out of place at that moment. When he spoke at last, it sounded as if he was hissing the words at her!

"What is wrong now? Why can't you ever be on time?"

"Excuse me!" To say that she was stunned was definitely an understatement. She looked at him to make sure that maybe his words were not as rude as she might have imagined them to be, but his face was becoming redder by the second, and he was becoming angrier than she'd ever seen him before. Snapping at his cousin and telling her to wait outside, Fadi then turned to Danya again.

"Really, Danya, first you could not do this alone, so you had your friend help you, then she is late, and now we're all late for no good reason."

Danya found her voice, "What on earth are you going on about, Fadi? The wedding ceremony starts in ten minutes...I am not late, and Zaara has nothing to do with this, it's bad enough you never thanked her for helping out!" Danya was outraged herself by now, but Fadi did not back down either.

"Father Alexander moved the ceremony. Your friend knows about it, so you are both late now. Just be done and hurry up."

And he actually turned his back on her and slammed the door going out! She was beyond furious, and was thinking of some choice words she had for him after the ceremony, but then she was trying to remind herself that what Zaara had told her once might be true. Maybe this was a stressful time for Fadi as well, he just did not know how to express his feelings in better ways, so steadying her breath, taking a last look at her reflection in the mirror, and hoping that people would think that the redness of her cheeks was from all the excitement of the wedding, she went out. Rami, Fadi's uncle, waiting for her by the door, holding her arm he escorted her on. Walking down the aisle, looking up into Fadi's face, Danya saw him smiling, but his smile did not reach his eyes... and she saw nothing. There was no love, no compassion... not even respect. With each step she was taking, her chest seemed to be closing in, like she could not breathe. And Danya realized she was making the biggest mistake of her life, she felt like she was ending her life, instead of beginning a new chapter. And she stopped.

She could hear people murmuring, but she was just standing there, in the middle of church, mid her own wedding, and was just staring at Fadi. And she was thinking fast. *Where does love go? How can you just stop loving somebody?* But that was exactly the feeling that went back and forth between her and Fadi....there was no love left. She let go of Rami's arm, she turned.... and she ran! She was running as fast as she could, people started calling her back—Fadi was yelling out her name— but she ran faster than even she knew she could run. It must have been a mile, but soon she was standing outside the coffee house, and she went inside. There were only a couple of customers in there, and they were looking at her as if she had the word 'crazy' tattooed to her forehead. Jeff, the other manager, came up to Danya, and offered her a seat and something hot to drink and calm her down. She was struggling to catch her breath, and shivering from head to toe.

"I just need to catch my breath, wait here for a little bit, until Zaara comes to pick me up."

"Does she know you're here, or would you like me to call her for you?"

"No, she does not know. Could you please call her for me?"

She sat in her corner booth, drinking the hot chocolate quickly to try and calm her nerves. She was not going to her house since that would be the first place everybody would be looking for her at. Luckily, Fadi never took interest in her friends, well, her only friend really, Zaara, so he had no access to her number or even address. Hopefully he won't think about coming and looking for her or Danya at the coffee house.

Ten minutes later Zaara was there. She was dressed up also, and even though she looked quite surprised to see Danya, there was something in her eyes that told Danya she was almost expecting this, then again, she did meet Fadi, and in all the times that she had met him, he treated her like a maid, not a maid of honor, and was ordering her around as if he was doing her the biggest favor in the world by having her help out with the wedding. *Come to think of it, lately Fadi almost thought he was doing the world a favor just by being here on the same planet with the rest of us mortals!!* "Come on, let's take you home." Zaara was saying to her.

"But I don't want to go to my house. They'll be there by now." And she shivered just thinking about it. Zaara patted her gently on her hand and said reassuringly. "Sorry, I meant my house. Come on let's go before more people come and start ogling us in these dresses. We do look ridiculous, you know."

Danya actually laughed with relief, and hugged her friend. That was what she was feeling, relief—no more anger, no more frustration...well, maybe a bit of both, but also a great sense of freedom, she was finally going to be her own person.

An hour later they were sitting in Zaara's living room, having a nice cup of tea. Danya was wearing a pink sweat suit that belonged to Zaara, her wedding dress lay in a heap on the bathroom floor, she was considering burning it up. *A bonfire party does not sound too bad right now! Shame I lost the shoes somewhere while I was running! That would have been a real 'closure' to this sad relationship.* Zaara was talking about what she still had left to pack of her things, since she was leaving to India within two days. There was a lot of excitement and happiness in her face, Danya shook her head in wonderment, and said as if more to herself than to Zaara. "I still don't understand! But then again today I don't understand a lot of things."

"What don't you understand? You just got away from a bad marriage—I'm getting married to a great man from a good and wealthy family, whom my parents approve of, and I am fond of. I am looking forward to marrying Rohan. I think our match is going to be a really good one."

"But... Devdas was your first love, and if he still loves you! There is no love—not anymore, between Fadi and me, honestly speaking, I don't know if I had ever been in love with him."

Zaara came and sat next to Danya, and was talking to her as if to a stubborn child. "You have to understand, things are done differently where I come from. It can be the

31

fiftieth century, and my parents would still be the same, my culture would still be the same, and I feel okay with it. I have to marry Rohan. Never mind that, I want to marry Rohan."

"But Devdas..." Danya argued on and was stopped by the look on Zaara's face.

Zaara sounded irritable now as she got up and said, "Dev has to grow up and move on. I will always hold him in my heart, but it is a different type of love than the one that is going to get me through a lifetime of marriage, and when I start my own family, I want my marriage to have a solid ground." She laughed a bit bitterly before adding, "You know, you sound like Devdas sometimes. He's actually the reason I was late today. He heard about my marriage being arranged, so he shows up and tries to convince me that I am making the biggest mistake of my life! He even suggested we elope today! I have no idea what has gotten into him. He was always such a level headed person."

Shaking her head, Zaara got up and went about packing the rest of her belongings. Danya was just sitting on the sofa, not thinking about her would-have-been husband, or the mess she was leaving behind. She was thinking about Devdas. Something about his face was haunting her. She was sure that no matter what Zaara was saying, Devdas was still in love with her, and he was not going to give up easily on their love if he was willing to travel all the way to the states just to convince Zaara to elope with him. *I don't even know the man, but I think I know his true feelings? Yeah, this is not crazy at all!!*

Zaara left on Tuesday, and Danya had to take care of some details before she left on Friday. She had to turn in her book, so she called her agent, Blake, and told him to take care of things for her while she was gone, like the book and even her house. She was planning on enjoying her stay in India as much she could before coming back to face the chaos.

On Friday morning she ventured back to her house, and again was lucky that there was no sign of Fadi there. She was packing her last bag when she decided she should call him to try and leave on a good note—or almost. *There's nothing wrong with optimism!* "Really Fadi, I am not blaming you or the world that I could not stand up for myself before. I should not need anybody to defend me—maybe I would not have so much anger and hatred inside of me if I only could have gotten to my feet and dealt with the reality of things a long time ago, I'm only sorry we did not resolve this a long time ago, we could have saved ourselves so much anger and heartache."

But how do you control the rage that builds up inside when you have no healthy outlet for any of it? She was thinking as some of that anger was boiling close to the surface now, but still she did not voice it out. Instead, she said. "To you Fadi, everybody else comes first, always. I don't even count most of the time."

She was throwing some clothes in a handbag, while she was talking on the phone— and becoming more agitated all over again. It was lucky for Fadi that he was not in front of her at that moment. She was thinking about how satisfying it would be to punch him to pulp! *Talk about becoming violent!*

"You have to listen to me Danya. You are acting on your anger and frustration, and..."

"No Fadi, you need to listen to me for once and hopefully for the last time. I cannot go through with this, and I cannot go through this again. I am only sorry I did not realize this earlier. Have you ever stopped and listened to what I was saying to you about our relationship? I mean, really listened instead of just nodding your head to whatever I was saying just so you could shut me up!"

"What was there to listen to? You always had doubts about us, since day one all you could talk about was ways of ending this relationship instead of how to build it." And now he sounded snappy too. Sometimes it was nice to realize he was not as 'bland' as he seemed most of the time!

"This is what I am saying, Fadi, since day one I told you we lack an essential thing in this pathetic excuse for a relationship and it is communication... yes, I talk, but you neither listen to what I say nor talk to me. It is worse than being alone... at least when I'm alone, I know it and I don't have to worry about what you will say or think, or worse, have to play the guessing game of trying to figure out what you are feeling or thinking. You wore me down...you nearly broke my hopes down...and now I have to figure things out for myself on my own."

Fadi snorted, and said sarcastically. "What you're saying is that you are going to India to live out some childish dream of yours, and you expect me to be okay with it."

Danya heaved a deep sigh, and prayed for one last drop of patience. "You are not listening to a word I'm saying, and this lack of respect for my feelings makes me realize that it was silly of me to bother and explain anything more to you. What would it take for you to wake up and realize that I don't expect you to be okay with this because I am done expecting anything from you? I am done talking to you now. Please have the decency to never try calling me again. I do wish you a happy life Fadi, goodbye." And she hung up without waiting for Fadi's reply.

Four
Namaste my India

'At a young age we are taught a lousy philosophy in our family, even maybe our culture and religion: every person that is rude to us has an excuse for his or her behavior, like the rest of the world has problems, and we are the only problem-free people on this planet! I've come to realize that this is the philosophy of the weak—nobody has the right or the excuse to cause another human being pain, whether physical, mental or emotional.'

Danya leaned back in her plane seat, and read what she had written on her notepad, maybe it was time she changed her path, even if for a bit...and for the billionth time that day, thanked the heavens that she had the ability, mental and financial, to just pick up and leave. And it made her think of all the other people in the world who would be stuck for the rest of their lives just because they did not have the means to pick up and run as fast as they could.

She closed her eyes, and slept soundly until the captain announced they were landing.

"Welcome to India, we hope you enjoy your stay here."

Zaara was at the airport to receive her, and gave her a big ecstatic hug as she almost lifted her off the ground. They both laughed happily. "You're here. Finally hah!"

"I know! I cannot believe I'm finally here. The first thing I thought of doing was to shout: 'Namaste mera India' at the top of my voice, but I'd figured they'd drag me off to check my brain, or even to check if I have one to begin with at this point."

Zaara led her friend out, laughing with obvious joy. "I see, so it's your India now! And how was your flight?"

"It was great, thanks to your planning. I actually enjoyed my flight so much I thought up a chapter for my next book: 'How to spot a jerk, and not marry him'."

Zaara laughed some more, helping Danya with her handbag, and said, "You are definitely on a roll. So I take it you talked to Fadi before leaving?"

"Ugh......."

"I'll take that as a yes, and obviously you did not accomplish much with that talk."

"Nothing at all, except to solidify how much we dislike each other and that we are definitely better off without each other. I still wish we'd figured this out sooner."

They got into the back seat of the shiny black Mercedes that belonged to Zaara's family, while Raj, Zaara's family driver, got into the driver seat, and they were on their way. Looking out of the window, Danya could not believe the beauty of a country she loved without visiting once.

"You look like you're deep in thought." Zaara said as she leaned back and enjoyed the view herself, there was no denying it, and her country was gorgeous. Danya turned to her with a content smile.

"I was just thinking how beautiful this all is, way beyond my imagination....and also thanking God above again and again that I could do this. I was thinking about this on the flight here, you know, that I am lucky to be able to pick up and leave whenever, and how I should do something to help other people, mainly women, who are in really bad situations, and I know there are many that are in way worse situations than mine. Like I said, at least I could run away, in a sense."

"That's a great idea, and I would love to help you make it happen when you really decide on it. Now, look around you and enjoy this...you're finally here."

"It is all so breathtaking! I feel as if I've known this country from another lifetime and now I'm remembering it all once again." Danya was trying to take in everything around her—the view, the people, the colors, the smells... everything. Everything was so very different in an exciting way. She was trying not to blink so as not to miss anything.... and Zaara was looking at her happily.

"So, is it all that you thought it would be?"

"Absolutely not... it's more! Much, much more than I had ever imagined it to be. I don't understand why Hindi cinema filmmakers would even go to foreign countries to film their movies when they have such colorful and exotic scenery here around them."

Zaara gave another light hearted laugh, and Danya turned to look at her closely. She truly was looking happy and content—at ease with life. And she asked her. "So, did you get to see Rohan since you got back?"

"Oh, yes. He actually came to receive me at the airport

with my parents. He got me a beautiful red rose, and a huge box of chocolates, and you know how I'm a big fan of chocolate. Believe it or not, I was very happy and excited to see him."

"And?" Danya wondered.

"And what Danya?"

"You are still sure about all of this?" Then she added as she saw the frustrated look on Zaara's face. "I mean, after coming back here and seeing Rohan in person, that is."

"Danya, look at me! I am the happiest I have ever been, so stop worrying yourself over nothing, and look out the window, you are missing out on my beautiful country. I am only sorry you missed the Sagai ceremony—you would call it engagement or ring ceremony."

"Oh, I know! I have so much to learn still Zaara. You have such beautiful names for all sorts of ceremonies and occasions."

Zaara's house was like a magical place to Danya. She was craning her neck to take in all the details, the furniture, the gardens, everything was so very different from the things she was used to in the states, even in Jordan, and much more extravagant. There were a lot of golden hues everywhere she looked and it did not look overdone, just perfect. And it was so spacious, it might have been a mansion, but as Zaara told her, it was a 'bungalow'.

"Your house is so beautiful, Zaara, I cannot believe you actually could live in your apartment back in the states after living in this gorgeous place all your life."

"Yes, it is beautiful, but I needed to finish my studies, and have the time alone. You know, to have some independence for a while before coming back to my roots."

It made no sense to Danya that Zaara could be so

liberated and yet so old fashioned, but she did not want to bring up the subject again, as it was beginning to irritate her. Zaara was looking very happy, content, and sure of her life right now, and that was all that mattered.

Zaara's parents turned out to be a great surprise, also. Instead of being cold, uptight and distant as Danya had imagined them to be, they were so welcoming, and so sincere that Danya felt accepted before they even sat down for tea. They were very interested in her as a human being not just as Zaara's friend, or a visitor from a different country, but as a person, period.

"You know what is so amazing?" Danya said to Zaara as they were on their way to the market to finish their last minute shopping before the celebrations were to start the next day. "All of a sudden my life before coming here seems like a dream, like I was always meant to be here! Crazy, hah!"

"No, you are in India now, so it's 'pagal'."

They had a pleasant time as they looked at some bangles and accessories. Everything was just so colorful and elegant. Danya bought some bangles and earrings, before she turned to Zaara.

"I'm going to the sweets shop that we passed on the way here. I can't wait to try some of the stuff they have in the window. Would you like to come with me?"

"No, you go ahead. By the way, here is a mobile phone for you to use while you're here, my number is already saved in there, so call me if you need anything, or if you can't figure out your way back." Danya kissed her on the cheek as a thank you, and then went to the sweets shop. Everything in there looked so different even from the Indian sweets she had already tried before. She picked one of the boxes that had a mixture of assorted sweets, and stood in line to pay for it, but she could not resist trying one of the sweets that were in the box...big mistake, she picked one of the besan laddus and as soon as she bit into it, she gagged!!!

The poor guy in front of her got the worst of it on the back of his suit jacket, and she mumbled to his back. "I am so sorry...so......."

But the rest of her words were lost as he turned around, and with a look of disgust on his face, looked at her. But his shock was nothing compared to hers, she nearly dropped the rest of the sweets on the already dirty, sticky ground. "Oh my God...Devdas!!!"

Of all the millions in India, she pukes on Devdas! Confusion now mingled with disgust on Devdas' face, he asked her while taking his jacket off. "I'm sorry, do we know each other?"

He was shorter than she had expected, but still taller than her five foot four. *Oh great, he's even much better looking than his picture!* She blushed as she said. "I... I'm sorry. I'm Zaara's friend from America... I'm here for the wedding." She could not help but notice a shadow of anger and sadness in his gorgeous eyes, but it was there only for a moment, and then he had the most astonishing smile on his face, stunning dimples and all. She was standing there, staring up at him like she'd never talked to a man before in her life! Or even seen one for that matter! Even his voice sounded exotic to her ears. *Oh, I'm so in trouble!!!*

"So you are here for the wedding. That's good." He commented as a worker from the shop brought a mop and some towels, and Danya finally took her eyes off Devdas, and tried to help the man, to try and get away from those blazing eyes, but the worker would have none of it, probably just wanting to get her out of the shop as quickly as possible.

So after mumbling apologies to every single person in the shop, and paying for her sweets, she left the shop, accompanied by Devdas, who for some reason or another decided to hold her under the elbow and walk her out.

"I can walk...I'm fine, really. I just did not expect the texture and the sweetness of the laddu." She glanced at his jacket, and tried to take it out of his hand. "Please let me take this and clean it off for you."

But instead he kept on walking, and asked her shortly. "Where is Zaara?"

"She's right there in that jewelry place. You don't have to come in there with me."

Danya sounded nervous even to herself, and she was not surprised that he raised an eyebrow looking at her sideways with curiosity. "Why, I would love to say hello to her and wish her luck." She was looking at him, while trying not to stumble and make a bigger fool of herself in front of this man...what in the world was wrong with her legs! And then the words blurted out of her mouth before she could even think. "Are you coming to the wedding?"

"I would not miss it for the world."

He certainly looks fine for a man whose beloved is marrying someone else. Danya was thinking she really should reconsider her ideas about love and marriage. Zaara was always telling her that she was too much of a dreamer. As they were walking to the jeweler's, Devdas seemed more interested in Danya.

"So you are from America?"

"Yes, that is where I met Zaara." That seemed to please him for some reason, and Danya kept on talking to ease her tension. She tried hopelessly not to sound so breathless and nervous. "She used to manage a nice coffee shop and we met there and became friends. She invited me to her wedding, and I always wanted to come and visit India, so that was a great opportunity for me... and now I'm here. Your country is very beautiful."

At those last words, he had a genuine smile on his face, and bent his head to tell her.

At those last words, he had a genuine smile on his face, and bent his head towards her saying, "I would not want to be anywhere else in the world. So are you here for long?"

Danya was looking up at him again in awe, and could not bring herself to tell him anything about escaping her own wedding to be there, add to that the fact that she really did not know the man! She was shocked at how familiar he looked, and how she could not remember what Fadi's 'perfect' features looked like!!

"This is actually my first trip to India, and I was going to stay for two weeks, but now I think I might be staying a bit longer, you know, to explore as much about this country as I can. Who knows when I would be able to come back here again?"

"Well, then we have to make the best of your trip to India. There is so much to see to only be here for two weeks, not to mention you would be busy with the wedding for a week."

She was admiring his use of the word 'we', when she realized that Zaara was again right about her, she was a dreamer, a hopeless one for that matter, with a wild and at times, extremely crazy imagination.

"By the way, I don't know your name." She heard him say.

"Oh yeah, I'm sorry. It's Danya...Danya Shadid."

"Pleasure to meet you Danya. I have to say, that is an unusual name for an American."

"I'm actually....."

But Devdas was no longer listening, at that moment they saw Zaara heading towards them with shopping bags in her hand. She was blushing from all the excitement, and possibly from meeting Devdas, but aside from that she was looking comfortable, at ease, and happy.

"How in the world did you two meet?" She wondered as she handed Danya her bag.

Telling Zaara about the incident at the sweets shop, Danya was watching both of them carefully. After shaking hands with Zaara, Devdas turned his attention to Danya again.

"Would you ladies like to join me for a cup of tea? There is a place nearby that serves great tea biscuits with their chai."

Danya looked at Zaara for the answer, she did not want to accept the invitation, and maybe make her friend uncomfortable, and yet she did not want to leave Devdas... not yet. Zaara was still smiling, and nodded her head okay. So Danya said yes to tea with a big smile.

The place they went to was pretty nice, and Devdas ordered some tea and biscuits. They sat on the patio watching the shoppers and enjoying the nice cool breeze, it was such a beautiful day.

"How are your wedding preparations going?" Devdas asked casually. Zaara looked taken aback for a second, but she was still smiling happily as she wiped her mouth with the napkin and answered.

"Real well, thank you for asking. My parents almost had

everything ready for me. I just needed to take care of some minor details. Are you coming over tomorrow night?"

That was the first moment Danya felt uncomfortable. Devdas took a minute to answer, but then smiling he said that he was not going to miss it. "If you really are still going through with this marriage that is." He added as if he was joking.

Zaara was giving him the same stern look she gave Danya when she asked about the same subject, but she was quite calm when she said firmly. "Of course I am. It's is for the best, for everyone."

As if a curtain fell over his face, Devdas smiled broadly, and lifted his cup of tea, as if he was toasting Zaara and Rohan, and said. "Congratulations, then, and best of luck."

It was nice and easy talk afterwards, about childhood and mutual friends, until it was time for Zaara and Danya to head back home, and Devdas walked them out of the café.

"I will see you both tomorrow night." He was saying as he held onto Danya's hand long enough for her to feel warmth spreading up her neck again, and she could not but gaze into his stunning eyes for as long as she could—she had never seen a more beautiful shade of brown in her life than the color of those eyes. She shook her head in wonderment and said shyly as she reluctantly pulled her hand away.

"Goodbye Devdas. And thank you for the tea."

"I will see you tomorrow night." He said as if he was making her a promise. As Danya walked away with Zaara, she kept looking over her shoulder, almost tumbling down on her face if Zaara had not held her arm at the last second, and asked, "What has gotten into you?"

"Zaara—how can you marry anybody else?" Danya

wondered breathlessly. Instead of looking bored with the question as she should, Zaara burst out laughing, grabbing Danya's arm and leading her into their waiting car, she said slyly. "So you fell under my charming friend's spell! Not shocking in the least. He is a very good looking man. But now I need you to stop your daydreaming and hurry so we can make it home for lunch, believe it or not, I'm still starving."

Patting Danya on the arm jokingly when they sat in the back seat of the car she added, "And please just stick to bread at my wedding." They were laughing as they entered the house some ten minutes later, carrying their shopping bags in with them.

Danya was thinking how her whole attitude towards life had been changing fast within the last week and how she herself was acting more like a teenager with a crush than the adult she is. After they had lunch and tea with the family, she went strolling in the garden, and was soon followed by Zaara. Danya seized the opportunity to apologize to her friend. "Zaara, I really want to apologize for the way I have been acting lately. I have no idea what has gotten into me all of a sudden. You know, I have always been more mature than my years, and yet now that I'm older I am acting like I just turned thirteen!"

Zaara smiled and handed her a cup of chai, while she sat down with hers. "I think it is because you never fully lived your teenage years, you had to grow up fast overnight when your parents passed away—you were on your own— and all the stress you were under lately is probably finally catching up with you. I'm just glad you're here and we can deal with it together. But don't worry...if anything, you know, like in case you happen to lose your head completely, I will just stuff a laddu in your mouth and wizen you up."

Laughing, Danya raised her arms in surrender. "Please, anything but those sweets for me." And they both spent the rest of the day looking through Zaara's shopping and trying on different accessories, it was such a different event from when Danya was getting ready for her wedding, that was a disaster waiting to happen, this was absolute joy, and the prospect of seeing Devdas again just added to that joy. Never in her life had she enjoyed herself more, and Danya was feeling grateful and thankful to all that she was receiving from her friend and life in general at that moment, rarely had she felt so serene, calm and content.

Five
Heartache for one

It was during the Sangeet ceremony, the dance and music party the next day that Danya realized that maybe she was not mistaken about some of her doubts about Devdas after all. Rohan was as wonderful as Zaara had said, and extremely handsome, Danya was finding it hard to deny that a man like him is a gem and being married to him would absolutely make Zaara's life the dream she herself was wishing for. But Devdas was still worrying her. The night started out with great food, a nice blend of vegetarian and non-vegetarian dishes that Danya sampled with joy, and wonderful lively music. The guests were wearing the most beautiful clothes anyone could have imagined, and again the colors were everywhere, men in traditional clothes from black to gray to brown, and the women outfits, whether saris or salwars were just a garden of vibrant colors: red, pink, blue, and silver. Just plain stunning. Danya was clicking away with her camera happily, and then she heard somebody ringing his glass to make a toast. She was making her way back towards Zaara and Rohan, when she realized it was Devdas who was speaking— and loudly.

"I would like to toast the happy couple, may you both have a great life together, and may you never remember the hearts you have broken to have your happy moments." Throwing back his drink, he threw the glass on the ground where it shattered into a hundred pieces, and the whole place was so quiet the tinkling of glass could be heard all around—Devdas turned and was storming out, when he saw Danya standing with her mouth open with shock, and headed towards her. He placed his cold palm on her cheek, which sent a shiver down her spine, especially when he said in a kind whisper.

"May you never suffer heartache in any of your lifetimes. I would not wish that on anybody... ever." And he walked out with everybody looking at him with mixed emotions, between anger, concern....and even pity. Danya looked at Zaara, who was shaking her head at her, while talking quietly to Rohan. She was looking annoyed and a bit embarrassed, but not heartbroken and not even angry. Danya tried to blend in again and enjoy the party, but she could still hear Devdas's words—even stranger than that, she could still feel the coolness of his hand on her cheek.

After the party, while she and Zaara were changing their clothes, Danya turned to Zaara and asked with the most serious look on her face, "Zaara, did you ever see the movie 'Devdas'?"

And Zaara burst out laughing. Putting the last of her jewelry in their box, she turned to Danya, and holding her hand in hers, she answered, "You are too much of a dreamer you scare me sometimes. Just because Dev's name is Devdas like the man in the movie, that does not mean he is going to obsess about me or drink himself to death for me. He just had a drink too many tonight, that's what happens to people sometimes, and let me tell you, Dev does not normally drink at all. He's a big boy, he will be okay. I am more worried about you now and all this dreaming you do while you are supposedly awake. Life does not end just because we do not end up with our first love, and the first love is not the last one. I loved Dev for many years, and yet fell in love with Rohan in only days. Do you understand what I am trying to say here, Danya?"

"Of course...I am sorry. I have been a handful, but then again it feels like you have been taking care of me one way or another since the day we met."

"Do not worry your pretty little head about it, that is what friends are for, last I checked anyways! Now we need to be well rested for the henna party tomorrow."

Have you ever met a person that drew you like a butterfly to light, a man you just felt attracted and attached to without reason and for no reason, and you felt the need to hold him and keep him safe from the world? How crazy is that I should feel like this about a man I just met only yesterday!! Mad!

Danya stayed up late writing in her journal, and thinking about Devdas, she could see his tormented eyes and hear the pain in his voice... or was it the feeling of betrayal that he felt? She was thinking that Devdas would not be attending the wedding after all, and was proven wrong by mid morning. She was walking outside as usual in the garden, and saw him walking towards her like one of those Grecian statues coming to life, but much better looking, and he was holding a beautiful white rose. *Well, what did the Greeks know!*

"Good morning. I hope I am still welcome here after my behavior yesterday?" Handing her the rose with a glorious smile, he waited for her to sit down, and then sat down himself as they saw Zaara coming down the garden path holding two cups of chai, he stood up again and she greeted him cheerfully.

"I did not hear you driving up, how are you this morning Dev?" Devdas was looking at her, too, and taking her cue that they should not mention what had happened the night before, he smiled at her graciously and accepted her invitation to join them for tea. It was fortunate for Devdas that Mr. and Mrs. Malhotra were out with some of their relatives, for they were still unhappy about how he had behaved in front of their family and friends. They sat there for an hour, talking about everything and anything, staying on safe turf. Danya was a bit put off to learn that Devdas would not be attending the night's festivities, but will be there the day after for the wedding.

And then Devdas left for the day. Danya ran upstairs to the bedroom she was sharing with Zaara, and pressed the rose carefully in one of her books, sighing at how childish she was becoming. The Mehndi ceremony was a colorful and beautiful event with more great food and lively dance music. While Zaara was having her hands, arms and feet covered with designs of flowers and colored in, Danya got some designs on her hands also, and was having so much fun she wanted this experience to last a lifetime. *Especially Devdas.*

The second time Danya saw him was the day before the wedding itself. She was alone at the house—and Mili came into her room, telling her that Dev sir was waiting for her downstairs. She almost ran down the steps, stopping by the huge hall mirror for a second to fix her hair.

"Hi Devdas. What a surprise." She said extending her hand to him.

"I'm hoping a good one." He said with that smile, looking as handsome as ever, and Danya was flushed as she shook his hand. He held on to her hand as usual, and she was wondering what to do with her eyes. She tried to concentrate on his necklace, but it was only making her more aware of how beautiful his dark skin was—his body heat was drawing her like a magnet, she just wanted to hide in his arms....forget about Zaara, forget about Fadi... just forget about the world, for that matter, no matter how inappropriate or irrational that sounded. His sudden laugh brought her out of her trance. "I'm sorry for coming to see you without calling ahead of time."

Getting hold of herself, as hard as it was, Danya smiled at him. "Oh, it's alright, really. I'm just getting my things ready for the wedding, and packing away what I won't need for the remainder of my stay here."

"You are still leaving soon after the wedding?" He was leading her by the hand to sit outside. One thing she already noticed about Devdas is that he liked being outside. Mercifully, as soon as they got to the garden, he let go of her hand, and sat down in one of the chairs, while Danya sat down, trying to keep her voice normal.

"Yes, a week from tomorrow. I still have to call a tour agency or something, so I can do as much sightseeing as I can in pretty much five days."

"So you have not done any sightseeing at all since you got to India?"

"No, but I can't say I have not been enjoying my stay in the house. And all the wedding parties I've been to so far have been great. Everything is so different even in the household, I love watching everybody and everything and taking pictures especially of the gardens, they are just gorgeous. Zaara had mentioned that you have an office in New York. Do you plan on going there soon?"

"Not really, I used to run the office there, but now I have an office manager who runs things for me, I only have to go there twice a year, unless an emergency arises which thankfully has not happened in the past two years. No matter how much I like traveling abroad, I love being back here."

"I don't blame you. It's stunning here."

He was watching her with that mesmerizing look he always has in his eyes when looking at her. Now, Danya knew she was no beauty, all brains... not much though of late, but when comparing herself to Zaara and all the beautiful and elegant women she had been meeting since setting foot in India, she had to admit she was a very average looking person, medium height, fair skin, round face with a straight nose, and nice lips, but her eyes were the most beautiful feature in her face, emerald green and almond shaped. And yet, Devdas was looking at her with something close to interest, or even fascination!

"I am glad you are having a good time here, that my country did not disappoint you."

"Are you kidding me? Look at this place!" She blurted excitedly, to which he burst out laughing, and she was turning an even deeper shade of crimson.

"I look at it every day." He said kindly.

"You are so lucky." His face lit with a mysterious smile,

and leaning towards her, he whispered. "You could be lucky too." Then standing up, he added in a normal voice. "Well, I better take my leave now. I will be seeing you tomorrow night. Thank you for receiving me. Goodbye Danya."

He shook hands with her, and was walking towards the gates when he turned around and gave her one of his dazzling smiles. *My God, this man is making me lose whatever is left of my sanity! How can one look from him make me forget everything and everybody else in the world? I have no idea why I was getting married to Fadi in the first place! I only hope I would have some brains left when I leave here.*

The wedding was a completely different affair also, from the decorations to the flowers, strands of marigolds, jasmine and roses covered the whole front of the house, to the puja (prayers) and rituals themselves. Everything was all so new, nothing like Danya ever seen in a documentary or even any of the movies she was always watching. There was dancing and food all morning while the bride was getting ready, and every move Zaara did and every piece of jewelry she put on had a special sacred meaning. After Zaara got all decked out, she went downstairs surrounded by her mother, father and all the girls and women. Everybody sat around her until the formal procession of the groom's party arrived, to Danya's only disappointment, not on a white horse! Rohan was dressed up elaborately as well with a head turban, and then when everybody moved the procession to the wedding hall where it was all taking place, the priest started the Var Mala ceremony, where Zaara and Rohan exchanged huge flower garlands. Then they moved to sit under the Mandap—the sacred four pillars canopy—for the holy priest to perform the rituals and rites of the marriage. Danya noticed how everything had a meaning, how Zaara was seated on Rohan's left before the Pheras—performing of the seven vows around the sacred fire that are meant to strengthen their bond of love—and then she moved to sit on his right when they were done. Zaara had told Danya in the morning that she and Rohan had agreed that she would wear a traditional Mangalsutra—a black and gold beaded necklace with a diamond pendant—and that the necklace itself is a symbol of marital dignity and chastity, the bride would wear it all her life until her husband's death, and that it is like a promise from the husband that they will always stay together no matter what. Danya was sitting near Zaara's mother, listening to the priest continuously chanting the prayers as Zaara and Rohan walked around the sacred fire seven times, and was throwing flowers whenever everybody around her did, she did not understand a word of the prayers, but it was all making her feel at peace with herself and the world. Devdas of course looked like a real prince charming in his traditional clothes in black and white, and the looks he was giving her were making her heart jump out of her ribs, if that was possible.

Zaara was stunning in her bright red silk sari with the fine gold thread that adorned the edges. She had on the biggest nose ring that Danya had ever seen, with a beautiful delicate gold chain that connected it to a hair piece near her ear—and the bangles! Danya herself was wearing an elegant salwar, a two piece pant suit in black with fine silver designs around the edges. She felt very confident, and was flushed with her joy. The reception hall was also decorated so elaborately, with flowers and lights everywhere, and the waiters were walking around with trays of hors d'oeuvres, and some had trays of sweets that Danya pretty much ran away from. She was walking around the hall and taking as many pictures of the decorations, the guests, and the colors, when she noticed Devdas making his way towards her in his perfectly fitting black suit.

"You have to try this, here take a bite, I don't want you to get your hands sticky while you have your camera. Open wide." And he held up his hand. Sitting in his palm, she saw a piece of sweets, small and round like a cylinder, and covered in edible silver decoration. Then she looked up at him. Was he trying to make her sick on purpose so she would ruin the party for Zaara? But as she was looking into his glorious eyes, Danya figured, *who cares if they kicked me out of the wedding....out of India for that matter? If I could have Devdas look at me like that! And hand feed me himself— rat poison would not even be bad out of those hands.*

She took a bite with her eyes still looking deep into his, and found that she actually liked this particular type of sweets. "What is it?"

"It is a kaju roll, pretty much pistachios and cashews. What do you think?"

"Just wonderful, thank you." And she was not sure whether she was talking about the sweets or Devdas himself. She was watching him carefully, looking for any sign that he was not as comfortable with Zaara's marriage as he was letting on, but there was nothing but a warm smile, and mesmerizing eyes, nothing to indicate that Devdas was not accepting that Zaara had moved on—finally.

Zaara had asked Danya once to gift her with an Arabic dance for her wedding, and now she came looking for her and said, "Now it's time for my gift, I asked them to play some Arabic music for you. Break a leg kid."

Danya walked to the middle of the dance floor, with all eyes watching her, but she only had eyes for one person, and as the music played, she danced. She looked into Devdas's face, and just started singing to the music too. "My life has just begun, all the days before you are gone, whether my eyes are open or closed, yours is the only face I see, only face I know. And I lift my hands to the heavens above, and offer a prayer that one day I will be gifted your love."

She was singing in Arabic, and was sure nobody understood a word, she hoped, but nothing mattered to her, she was thinking how filmy she was being—just because she was in India, and they sang in most of their films did not mean that she had to sing her love for Devdas in front of five hundred people!! And then it hit her... she was falling in love, or was already in love with her best friend's first love!! Devdas had the most beatific smile on his face that almost made her cry, but she turned towards Zaara, who in turn nodded at her, and had a knowing smile on her face as she winked at Danya.

After the music stopped, Danya made her way to the other end of the hall, and tried to avoid Devdas for the rest of the night, she was beyond disturbed by her discovery, and she had a feeling he understood some of the words, or maybe the pathetic way she kept staring into his face whenever he was near? She only wanted the night to go by smoothly without her acting like a love-struck teenager. She danced with a couple of Zaara's relatives, and even danced with Devdas once, but got away from him as soon as the song ended.

Zaara and Rohan left after the party, and even that had its own ceremony—Vidai ceremony—a post wedding ceremony, where the bride is accompanied by her parents and friends and family. Everybody walked her to the doorstep, where she threw back three handfuls of rice and coins over her head into her parents' house, as a symbol of repaying her parents for all that they have given her before, and as a ritual to keep wealth and prosperity intact in her home. Danya was standing there with everybody, throwing rice at the bride and groom, who were leaving in the early morning for their honeymoon in England. Mrs. Malhotra explained to Danya that they threw rice and rose petals over the couple's heads for good luck, and that rice was a symbol for a new prosperous life. Zaara came looking for her before they left. "I will call you, Danya. Please try and stay until we get back next week. I would love to have you staying with us for a while."

"I will try my best. You take care of yourself, and have fun."

The two friends hugged briefly, before Rohan came and thanked Danya for being there for their wedding, and insisted on her staying with them once they got back. And then the bride and groom were gone with everybody now throwing coins after their retreating decorated car to ward off any evil.

Danya went to her bedroom, was thinking of going to bed, when her cellular phone rang!

"Hi Danya. It's Devdas." She was not expecting this. She sat down on the bed and held the phone closer to her ear, she almost stopped breathing just to try and hear 'him' breathe. "Hello, Devdas."

"Sorry to have called you at this hour, but tomorrow I have a business meeting in the morning and then I'm heading for another in Amritsar, it would only take me an hour. If you like, you could come with me. We can fly out there and be back around nine at night. We can go visit the golden temple, if you have nothing planned for tomorrow that is."

"Oh, I would love to, if it won't be too much trouble."

"No trouble whatsoever. See you at eight thirty."

"That would be perfect."

Danya had a sleepless night; tossing and wondering what on earth had gotten into her to sing to a man she just met a couple of days before that she was in love with him. Maybe he understood some of the words—after all some Arabic and Hindi words did sound the same and had the same meaning, or maybe it was just the silly way she had been acting around him, she would not make a fool out of herself when they go to the Temple, she will try her best to look and act like the adult she is. She was hoping, anyways.

At exactly eight thirty Devdas was waiting for her outside. She had told Zaara's parents about her plans for the day, and they just wanted their guest to have the best time, so they had no objections to her going with Devdas.

When they got to the offices where he was having his meeting, he escorted her to a coffee shop in the same building, and made sure she was settled well before leaving her. Danya was enjoying being taken care of. It only took Devdas half an hour, before he joined her for a cup of tea and some sandwiches. They talked about the weather, the differences of climates between India and the states, nothing personal, but Danya was listening to every word out of his lips. *After all, this is the most insane memory I will have of India, how I fell in love with my friend's first love!* Looking into his face and just thinking of never seeing him again was tearing at her insides. She must have teared up, because Devdas stopped talking, and tilting his head he leaned closer to her, placing his hand onto hers. "Are you okay?"

Recovering fast and not wanting his hand to ever leave hers, yet again as pathetic as that was. She looked at the table top, not really seeing it, and muttered in a choked voice, "Yeah, I'm fine, just remembered something—something back home in America."

"Well, I hope you always have happy memories of India, nothing that would bring tears of sadness into your eyes ever."

"Thank you." Taking a sip of water, she willed herself to calm down.

"Are you ready?" And he helped her out of her seat and back into his car. Danya was looking out of the window as Devdas drove, not seeing anything, and for once not paying any attention to what she was supposed to be looking out for, when Devdas pointed to a street vendor who had a cart full of flowers.

"We should get you one of these flower necklaces. Marigolds are the most popular ones of all, and I believe they are a sign of good fortune."

"You really don't need to get me anything, thank you though. I really appreciate you taking the time to show me around. This is very kind of you."

"It's my pleasure, and I insist." He said with that heart melting smile, and Danya could not bring herself to look into his face, she kept tearing up. *So much for not making a fool out of myself today!*

Devdas stopped the car, and talked to the flower seller, and then paid him. He handed her the pretty necklace of yellow and orange marigolds, and she held them to her chest like a valuable treasure. She was having a hard time not crying in front of Devdas, which would probably be the last straw for him.

"I cannot imagine having to leave here in five days—Zaara asked me to stay longer, but there is so much that I need to take care of back in America, I'm already behind schedule on so many things."

"What do you have to go back to, if you don't mind me asking? Do you have a boyfriend or relatives waiting for you over there?"

"None actually, but—I don't know. I am not always like this, really. I almost always know what I am doing and when, but lately it feels like my life is running way ahead of me and out of my hands, instead of me trying to run my life." Danya gave a quiet sigh, and looked back out of the window, her vision still blurry, and she was scared of how emotional she was becoming—just because! It felt like she had no control over what she was doing or saying anymore.

"I guess I'm just sad to leave here so soon. It's been a long time since I felt this happy."

"So don't leave." He suggested calmly. Danya turned to him now, and smiled into his face.

"I wish it could be this easy—there is nothing I would like more right now, but..."

He surprised her by reaching over and holding her hand, and saying with the same serious tone. "No buts. Stay here and marry me."

Danya was sure of her insanity by now; Devdas could not—would not ask her to marry him so simply! "Excuse me...what!?!?!"

Devdas parked the car, and turned towards her, with a stunning smile shining his whole beautiful face, his provocatively stunning dimple showing in his cheek that she was tempted to kiss, and reached out for her hands again. "Stay in India, and marry me today—now."

"Yes." Danya heard the word of approval coming out of her mouth, but could not believe what was going on. She figured God must be playing games with her, just to test her sanity, or what's left of it anyways.

They never made it to the golden temple that day, instead Devdas drove them to a near temple—Danya followed his lead as they were being instructed of what to do. Eloping was never one of her choices in life, and marrying out of her religion was always something she tried to avoid at all costs—but it all seemed so right at that moment—nothing and nobody else mattered. Looking into Devdas's face and realizing how much she loved him, Danya just thought it was so right, and absolutely the most romantic thing to do. Danya put the veil over her head, and followed Devdas around—and an hour later she was his wife.

Six
Happily ever after!

Cheer joy filled Danya's every being, but as they were driving back towards his family home, some reality began to settle in. *What would Zaara say? What would Mr. and Mrs. Malhotra say? And why was Devdas being so very quiet?*

Devdas had a blazing look in his eyes, not a happy one, but an unnerving look that was making Danya more nervous than she already was. "Is everything alright, Devdas?"

"Just perfect." His answer did not reassure Danya's thoughts or worries. There was definitely coldness about him. He was too quiet; he did not try and hold her hand, nor look at her since they left the temple. Devdas looked very detached. As soon as they reached his house—her house now— he finally held her hand, pulling her out of the car, and practically ran with her inside, yelling, "Ma! Mother!"

Mrs. Khanna came into the entrance with Devdas's

sister, Zohar, in tow, and they stopped in their tracks when they saw Devdas holding Danya's hand, with the red veil still covering her head, the vermillion that adorned the parting of her hair, and the marigolds around both their necks. Mrs. Khanna had a look of horror on her face. Then she recovered and was talking loudly and angrily to Devdas, but Devdas just sneered and listened, then he said shortly, in English for Danya's benefit. "This is Danya, my American Christian wife, and there is nothing to do about it now."

Even though she found Devdas's introduction of her odd, Danya was moving towards his mother to greet her, after all it was their first time meeting each other, neither she nor Zohar were at any of Zaara's parties, but Devdas grabbed her hand, and while she thought he was taking her to get his mother's blessings, he walked around his mother and sister, and was leading Danya upstairs. Danya looked back at his family, who were just standing there, staring at them with shock!

"Shouldn't I be getting your mother's blessings?" She wondered.

"No." Was his curt answer. *Maybe he wants us to freshen up first and dress more properly!*

Devdas walked her into what could only be called a suite. It was a beautiful living area, with a door leading into a great master bathroom, and another door that lead to two almost identical bedrooms. And then he said, "This will be our area of the house. Nobody else will have anything to do here, you can arrange and re-arrange whatever you like, and there will be a girl just to serve you."

Danya walked into the rooms, admiring their beauty, and still trying to understand Devdas's actions. She sat down at the edge of the sofa, not daring to look up at the man who had become her husband! Anybody who did not believe in love at first sight obviously had never met Devdas. She was thinking about how lucky she was, when her dream man delivered his next shocker of the night.

"You can pick whichever bedroom you like, I don't care, and to make things clear, we are going to have separate bedrooms. We will have to share the washroom, though. I hope that would not be a problem for you."

He was pouring himself a glass of water, not bothering to ask whether she wanted one also, as if what he just said to her was not strange at all. There was something definitely wrong going on, but she still could not put her finger on it. "May I ask you something?" She asked hesitantly.

"Might as well get it over with now. Ask away."

This is not right. What is wrong with Devdas? Danya was thinking, and yet she did not know how to put it in words without upsetting Devdas, but as she was trying to think of the best way to word her question, he asked impatiently. "Well, what is it Danya?"

And she blurted the first thing that came forth to her mind. "Why did you marry me?"

He turned to look at her with the crooked smile that only made his mouth more attractive, and she loved so much. She was staring at his lips, hoping for some reassuring words, she was unsettled by his attitude. "You are my mother's worst nightmare come true—you're perfect."

Not surprisingly, his last word did not seem to make her feel any better. He then added as if more to himself. "Have you ever promised to love somebody till the end of time?"

Finally managing to speak, her voice was more of a croak, Danya said. "Uh...Devdas, I really don't understand what's going on here? Are you really saying that you married me to spite your own mother?"

Smirking, he answered while looking at her still sitting on the edge of the sofa, with a look of shock, and possibly fear on her face. "I am not asking you to follow the rules of my culture, by all means, I prefer that you break each and every one of them. And to make it easier, you can call Zaara's parents and tell them where you are, and tell them to inform Zaara of our marriage."

"You're kidding me!!!" It was more of a whisper, but he heard her and asked. "Excuse me?"

Tears were rolling down her face, but she could not wipe them off, she could not even take her eyes off of him. May God help her, she loved Devdas, beyond reason, beyond sanity! And Devdas was just standing there, not saying a word, waiting for her reaction. Danya finally managed to stand up, although her legs were shaking, she walked with as much dignity as she could muster at that moment, and before entering one of the bedrooms, Danya turned to look at her husband, he obviously was still waiting for her to say something... a response.

"I will take this room. Let me know what my duties in this household are in the morning. I will need to be left alone until then."

After shutting the door as calmly as she could, she leaned with her back against it, eyes shut, but she did not cry. She was now shocked beyond tears. She was just realizing that Devdas had not once actually told her that he loved her... he had not lied to her. Yes, it was a weird punishment for Zaara and his mother to marry her, but he never once told her that he wanted to marry her because he loved her, or even asked whether she loved him! He simply said that if she loved the country she should stay and marry him. *Love the country—not love me, or love you—why did my pathetic brain register none of this before? Am I that naïve? Or the truth is that my feelings for Devdas are so strong that they covered for all other rational senses?*

Danya was not thinking of leaving. She could not run away from another relationship, this time an actual marriage. She made up her mind to stay, and maybe, just maybe, one day Devdas's heart would recognize her love for him, and maybe love her in return.

Maybe I am a hopeless romantic like Zaara says—oh, God. What is Zaara going to say when she finds out? Why had I not thought at all when I said yes to this crazy mess I got myself into?

After calling Mrs. Malhotra, and telling her where she was and why, and after dealing with her shock at the news, Danya then called Blake and told him that she was actually staying in India, and asked him to take care of the house and everything else for her. She gave him her number, and asked him to not give Fadi any details about her whereabouts. Blake informed her that Fadi had moved all of his belongings out of her house, and that he, Blake, had installed new locks. At least that part of her life was in order. Danya finally got herself into the bed. All of a sudden having separate bedrooms gave her a sense of relief, she would have died if she had to share a bed with her husband while she knew that he was in love with another woman, and was pining for her. She slept through the night, and she woke up to Devdas knocking on her door in the early morning hours, the sun was still waking up itself.

"Come in." Her voice was hoarse but composed.

She was standing next to the bed, trying to smooth

her clothes and hair as he walked in greeting her, "Good morning." Danya was looking for any sign that maybe the night before was just a cruel prank, but Devdas had no expression on his face as he walked to a chair and sat down. She replied with calm that she did not feel in her heart.

"Good morning Devdas."

"I came to tell you that you can go wherever you want in the house. Look around to get used to the surroundings, if you want to go shopping for clothes or anything else you might need, here is a credit card for you to use. The Malhotra's should be sending your things with my driver later on today. Do not try to deal with my mother or sister, stay away from them, Vidya will be your personal maid, ask her if you need anything, she speaks English." Danya was sure that her jaw had hit the floor.

"So you do not want me to participate in anything in the household, not the prayers, not the cleaning, not the cooking, nothing?"

"Exactly." And he actually smiled with satisfaction, then added, "Zaara should know by now of our marriage. Breaking one's relations is not as easy as she thought it was."

Choking on her words, but refusing to break down in front of him, she mumbled, "I don't know anything anymore." At which he was looking at her thoughtfully, and curiously.

"What did you expect, Danya? You know, when you said yes to this marriage, what was your motive?"

She knew she could not tell the truth, nor lie to his face, smiling sadly she turned away from him and walked to the window that overlooked the beautiful gardens. "Devdas, let's just say that all of this is not exactly strictly your fault.

I set myself up, in a way, from the beginning, I wanted to escape my boring life, so I built my own fantasy around your country, and as soon as I saw my 'escape', I took it without stopping to think. I am at fault, too. So let's just call it even and move on with our lives. Don't worry, I have no intention of leaving." And she turned around to move as far away from him as possible, she did not trust herself to be that close to him and not want to be in his arms—she was born to belong in those arms—and yet those arms did not want her, or want her love for that matter.

"I'm sorry you don't have a change of clothes with you, I'll make sure you have something soon. We'll be having breakfast in half an hour." And with that and a nod of his head he left.

What do you do when your life shatters? You pick up the pieces and move on.

Danya made sure to look like nothing in the world was bothering her as she made her way down to breakfast, there was not much she could do to her wrinkled clothes but she put on a brave face. To her luck, everybody was already there, they had just finished their morning prayers. She sat down next to Devdas, who smirked happily as his family eyed Danya with dismay. Zaara may not have been their choice of a bride, but Danya was obviously their nightmare, as Devdas had stated the night before.

Mrs. Khanna mumbled something to her daughter, and they hurried through their meal and got up before Danya was even finished with her tea. This seemed to please Devdas to no end, and made Danya feel as if she was swallowing rocks, not bread. She ate her piece of bread quietly, then rushed back upstairs.

After Devdas left for the office, Danya stayed in her

room, and after getting her bags, she took a long, relaxing bath before wearing one of her nicest dresses. *Just because I feel miserable does not mean I have to look it.* When her phone rang, she was wondering who would call her, and then she heard Zaara's voice which was full of excitement, pretty much screeching in her ear. "Congratulations! I could not believe it when my mother told me."

"Thank you Zaara—and sorry—I am truly sorry if I had betrayed our friendship in any way by doing this. . ." And her voice trailed off as Zaara's joyous laughter rang in her ears.

"What on earth are you talking about? Danya, this is great news. You should by now know there is nothing left of my story with Dev. I'm sure he told you that himself."

Sure—and this is why I'm in this mess now. But she could not bring herself to say it out loud. She only wished that Devdas could understand that Zaara was happy with her new life—and happy for them. "I'm glad, and relieved that you are okay with all of this."

"Of course I am, and Rohan sends you his regards and congratulates you both. We will be coming back in three weeks instead of next week. It turns out we have to go to New York. Rohan has some work there. But when I do come back, I will come and see you, so you can give me all the good details."

"Thank you again. Tell Rohan I said hello. Have fun, and I will see you when you get back."

Zaara laughed again, "Of course you will. Take care of yourself and give Dev our congratulations. Bye."

"Bye Zaara." As she hung up the phone, Danya noticed her trembling hands. What irony! Devdas wanted her to be Zaara's punishment, and Zaara was beyond thrilled

69

that her two friends have gotten married. She decided not to tell Devdas that Zaara had called, she could not handle telling him about Zaara's joy, or having him tell her what a wonderful punishment this was—but really, who was being punished here?

Danya could hear everybody else in the household keeping busy, whether in the kitchen or with the house chores. She went down to the kitchen, and without saying a word to anybody, she started helping the cook cut up the vegetables. Neither Zohar, nor Mrs. Khanna said anything to Danya, but at the same time they were not being rude to her as she had feared, or Devdas had hoped, like they decided they had to live with her just like she had to live with Devdas. They talked between themselves, and Danya was feeling a soothing comfort listening to a language she loved and did not understand much of.

As days went by, Danya found that she was settling smoothly into the Khanna household as if it was where she belonged all her life—she did not try to talk to Mrs. Khanna or Zohar, not even the help, except for Vidya. But even Mrs. Khanna was becoming more accepting of her, not with words, but by not mumbling anymore when she was around. Danya was getting used to her new life, she never went out with Devdas to any social events, she actually barely saw Devdas or talked to him except in the evenings, when he was trying to parade how different she was from his own family, but he was also noticing that she was more settled in the house, and his mother and Zohar were kind of more accepting of her. That did not look like it was making him happy in any way.

Neither of them mentioned Zaara's name, and Danya was always keeping an eye out to see if Devdas might show any signs of self-destruction that she associated with his name, luckily, there were none.

As for her writing, it was going very well, she already called Blake to give him the good news that she would be sending him the next book sooner that they had both expected, it was a short story. Blake was telling her that Fadi was calling him all the time to get anybody to tell him where she was staying in India, when Devdas walked in, and she hastily ended the call, promising Blake that she would call him back soon, and hung up the phone. Devdas did not say anything to her, he did not even look remotely curious. But then when he was about to enter his bedroom, he turned abruptly and asked her as if he had just thought about it. "Was that Zaara?"

She fought her urge to scream, and instead answered as if it had not bothered her, or broke her heart that he would be so interested in her calls only if they were from Zaara.

"No. It was one of my friends in America." She said shortly, and they left it at that.

Seven
New beginning...
or the end!

*O*n one rare occasion, they were sitting on the balcony of their suite, having some tea, while Danya was watching the sunset and reading a book, and Devdas was going through some work related papers. She kept sneaking looks at him, noticing how the fading daylight made his sharp features more prominent, the reddish golden glow of the setting sun reflected on the smooth shining blackness of his hair—the hair that her fingers itched to touch that they were actually tingling. She was wondering if she could sell a book just going on about how good looking her husband was! She smiled to herself and mumbled, "Pagal!" (Crazy)

Devdas looked up, and asked. "What?"

With her face flushed from her thoughts, she answered while looking at her laced fingers.

"Nothing, I was just mumbling—I do that a lot."

He put down his papers, and was looking at his wife with new interest, he asked with no trace of sarcasm. "You never told me you speak Hindi."

"I don't. I only know some words from the movies I watch. I honestly can't even tell the difference between Hindi, Punjabi or any other language and dialect."

And he smiled kindly at that. "Have you watched a lot of Hindi movies?"

Danya's face lit up, "I have always loved Bollywood movies, since childhood, really, but I still cannot understand a movie without subtitles. My grandfather took me to see my first Bollywood movie 'Coolie', when I was seven years old, and I have been attached to them since then." She laughed shyly and blushed before adding, "I actually wanted to marry Amitabh Bachchan until I was thirteen."

His smile widened, showing his dimple, and he wondered, "Which movies did you like best?"

Danya looked into those beautiful eyes, there was no contempt, no sarcasm—just real interest for a change, so she answered truthfully. "There are so many, but my favorites have to be 'Amar Akbar Anthony', 'Dil ne jise apna kaha', and... and 'Devdas'."

It was Devdas's turn to laugh in amazement, such a glorious feeling to hear him laugh, fills her heart with so much joy, and hope. "And now you have your own Devdas." And just like a light flickers off, so did his smile, which turned into that sneer.

"Sorry to disappoint you though, this Devdas is not going to die for any woman, or fall in love with another woman."

And he went into his bedroom, and made a big show of locking the door. Danya stayed in her seat, stunned at how Devdas could turn on her so fast. Ten minutes later Danya heard his car roaring off, and that was when she allowed herself to cry in silence. "This won't do—I'm a grown up, and it's time I start acting like one." She kept telling herself as she dabbed at her swollen eyes.

An hour later she was in the kitchen watching the cook, Poonam, and trying to pick up more Hindi and Punjabi words, when Zohar came in there looking for her.

"Ma*ji* told me to come and get you." It was possibly the first time that Zohar had addressed Danya in English, and personally. She had a harried look about her. Danya felt her heart skip a beat.

"What is wrong? Is ma*ji* okay?"

"It's Dev*bhai* (brother). He had a car accident. We are leaving for the hospital—hey, are you okay?" Zohar moved to hold Danya's arm, for she was swaying, she could not feel her legs anymore, but she held onto a chair for a moment, and then she was running out to the car, and Zohar was running after her. "Slow down, we are all going together."

The trip to the hospital felt like the longest Danya had ever taken, and once they got there, she could not contain herself. She wanted to find her husband. She had to make sure he was okay. Dr. Soud came to meet them in the waiting room, he explained a whole lot to Mrs. Khanna in Hindi, but she then turned to Danya and introduced her to the doctor. "This is my daughter-in-law, Dev's wife, she only understands English." At that the doctor addressed them all in English, and Danya was feeling grateful to her mother-in-law even through her worries.

"Is my husband okay—please? Tell me he's okay!" She asked the doctor pleadingly.

Danya was shaking, and Mrs. Khanna held her hand in hers. Dr. Soud smiled kindly, and continued talking to them about Devdas's condition. "As I was just saying to Mrs. Khanna, Mr. Khanna is going to be fine. He can actually leave today, if the x-ray results show there are no fractures. He will only have some bruises, and he had six stitches to the cut on his forehead. Honestly he is quite lucky. The car from what I heard is in a pretty bad shape."

"So he's fine—he's really, really alright?" Danya had to make sure. The doctor's smile widened.

"He really is fine. You can see for yourself. He is sleeping right now, but he should wake up soon enough." And he excused himself as the nurse came to escort her and his mother.

When they let her into his room, Danya wanted to check every hair on Devdas's head. She touched his bruises with gentle fingers—he was well! She was crying silent tears. "Thank God. Thank you Lord."

Mrs. Khanna came in to check on Devdas too, she did not stay long, but she gave Danya a gentle smile, and patted her arm. Before leaving the room she turned to her and said, "Dev is very lucky to have married you."

The hospital discharged Devdas, as the x-rays showed that he had no other injuries, and he went home with Danya who stayed behind waiting for him. When they got home, Mrs. Khanna helped getting Devdas settled in his bed, and went downstairs to supervise the dinner.

After eating some soup, and taking his medications, Devdas fell asleep with Danya sitting next to him, holding his hand. When she heard his steady breathing, she seated herself gently on the bed next to his legs, and just kept looking into his face. She was running her fingers through his hair, so black and soft—the beautiful eyes that never looked at her with more than contempt most of the time— the proud nose, the full lips, the strong jaw. . . She was having a strong urge to kiss every inch of his face, she fantasized about how it would feel to actually kiss those stunning lips, but would not dare. She could imagine the anger and sarcasm he would lash out at her for offering him something he never asked for in the first place.

Danya woke up to cold fingers touching her forehead, she had dozed off, and she was now leaning sideways onto the bed, over Devdas's legs, and still holding onto his hand. She looked up, and saw Devdas smiling down at her. Jumping off the bed, she smoothed her clothes, and said without meeting Dev's eyes.

"Hi, how are you feeling?"

Devdas cleared his throat, before saying hoarsely but kindly. "I feel fine, but my head feels funny though— heavy."

She moved closer to him again, and pointed out. "That's because you hit your head, and have some six stitches to your forehead. Do you remember the accident?"

He touched his hand to the bandages. "Not exactly, I seem to remember light, loud bangs and then sharp pain in my head. From what I heard at the hospital though, luckily, no other vehicle was involved, nobody else got hurt."

Danya was touched that he cared about the well-being of others. *Except for me, that is.* To him she said, "Would you like something to drink or eat?"

"I am thirsty. Can you have somebody make me a cup of chai please?"

She smiled at him, and said. "I will make it, and you should have something to eat, so you could take your medication .Would you like a sandwich or just biscuits?"

"I would like something light please, maybe just biscuits, thank you."

Danya was heading to the door when he laughed and said. "What's with the sudden kindness?"

She smiled back at him with all her heart. "Let's just say I'm glad you are well."

She prepared a tea tray and snacks, and went back up to the bedroom. She realized that for all the time they were together, she had never seen him in bed before. That thought brought color to her face, and she was still blushing as she entered Devdas's room. He was sitting up in bed, and his pajama top was not buttoned all the way up, so she could not take her eyes off his dark chest, and her color deepened.

"You look just like you scrubbed tomato paste all over your face. Are you okay?" He asked her.

Devdas seemed amused by her embarrassment. His chuckle startled her back to reality. She put the tray down, and handed him his tea, trying to keep her eyes averted from his.

What on earth is wrong with me? He probably thinks I have never seen a man before in my life! She finished her cup of tea while he ate a couple of bites, finished his tea, and then took his medications, Danya took the tray back to the kitchen, and then came back to help him get settled back in bed.

"Let me know if you need anything else. I will keep the doors open so I could hear you if you call out. Good night."

And she walked as fast as she could to her own bedroom without giving herself away.

Devdas's treatment changed dramatically after his accident. He was not exactly loving, but much nicer towards Danya. There was no more contempt in his words or actions anymore. They talked about her books, and how she wanted to change direction. Devdas said it was a great idea. "I don't know why you never told me before that you are a writer."

They were sitting outside. It was another nice day, and Devdas suddenly let out an amused laugh. Danya mused how it always sounds like music to her ears. *Pathetic!*

"And I just cannot believe you never told me before that you are an Arab-American, so much for giving my mother a culture shock."

"Well you never asked me about myself before, you only assumed what you wanted to suit you. But I am a Christian, so there is still a shocking element there if we are still going for that."

At which he laughed, and said, "I honestly think it is not working as well as I thought it would." And he changed the subject on purpose. "How's it going with the new book?"

"It is still all over the place, really, but I want to express how ridiculous it is that nobody pays attention to the little details that belittle us women. Take for instance in my country, if a woman gives birth to a girl, first thing most people say is 'Well, hope next time you can give your husband a boy', as if girls are not good enough! Or worse, as if the mother did not do her 'duty' properly, and she should be ashamed for not delivering the heir! And God forbid the woman is barren, then it is assumed she is at fault, that there's something wrong with her as a human being, and that her husband can either divorce her, or if he's a Muslim, he can marry another woman, but if the man was the one who could not get his wife pregnant, she should stay with him no matter if she wanted to be a mother or not! It is considered to be her duty! If a husband cheats, it is of course his wife's fault somehow, she was not enough for him, or she made him unhappy with her, but if the wife cheats, no matter how miserable her life with her husband could be, she is branded as a whore, pardon my french. I am against cheating whether it's the man or the woman doing it, if you're not happy get out, do not cheat, but why the double standard? Men can divorce their wives anytime they want to, but if a woman wants a divorce, it's not as easy, she has to move heaven and earth and maybe she would be granted her freedom from a miserable marriage and it still would be a maybe. Men can pick up and leave whenever they want whereas a woman needs to get her husband's permission to leave the country! It does not matter if a man chooses never to get married in his life, he's a sworn bachelor, but if a woman does not want to get married or have children, there has to be something wrong with her. A divorced man with kids can get remarried and there would be no problems at all, if a divorced woman with children decided to get married again, she could lose custody of her children! Absolutely ridiculous!"

Devdas was listening to her every word, with his head tilted to one side, and listening without voicing an opinion. Danya realized it was almost the same in India— well, almost all over the planet that girls and women were not as important for most people, and yet, looking at him, she realized he might just be different. She carefully asked, "Do I sound too harsh and bitter?"

He shook his head smiling "Not exactly, you do have big ideas about what's due to women, and since it's something you feel so strongly about, you should voice it out, so it does not build up into anger and resentment. The world is not always gentle, so it is okay to be harsh sometimes."

It astounded her how he could understand so much about her in a few words, while Fadi could not understand her long talks throughout all their years together. Warmth spread up her face, and she added more softly, "I do understand that it is not always the case, that there are wonderful men out there, also, and women who are just out of it, it's just the general morale of the society that bothers me to no end. Even though Jordan is one of the most beautiful countries in the world, and most of our traditions are great, very respectful and family oriented, some people have adapted these other disturbing beliefs, and for one reason or another, they are becoming the norm! It's a shame we don't show the world our greatness, only the bad seems to be taking center stage."

Nodding his head in agreement, Devdas said. "You should put all of this down on paper. By all means, we will try and get it published in Hindi, too. I agree with you that the whole world is becoming so advanced in technology and science, but at times they still have some backwards ideas when it comes to humanity and being humane."

Blushing with joy, she whispered a thank you, and restrained herself so she would not jump and kiss him full on that gorgeous mouth. They spent the rest of the day enjoying the gardens. They never left the grounds around the house, but she was just happy to have him for company, and enjoying the newfound camaraderie that was born between them. Another thing she noticed about Devdas was that he liked spending time with his family—if he was not at work, he was with them at home, not because he had to, but he seemed to really enjoy being with them. And he always showed interest in her progress with the new book. Marveling at the difference between the two men, Danya thanked the stars and God for her husband, at least he restored her faith in mankind on a different level.

She had once shown Fadi her new contract, and he laughed at the numbers, and before leaving to play golf with his friends, he said: "Well, we always knew you're no Danielle Steele." And he just had a look on his face, a look that conveyed that Fadi actually enjoyed trying to make Danya feel bad about herself, to put her down!

On another occasion Danya braved herself and asked Devdas if he was seeing anybody—it was eating at her peace of mind, and heart. He looked at her as if she was losing her mind. "I don't know what marriage means to you, but I do consider myself married to you, even if it's on paper and that would be adultery in my book."

She was very tempted to just go up to him and hug him as tight as she could, but she knew it was a little too soon in their new relationship to show her true feelings for him. He was looking at her curiously though. "What makes you ask such a question?"

"It is just something I remembered from before. Not about you, it is this guy I used to know, he was... umm... engaged to my friend and supposedly loved her, but he still cheated on her, twice, his excuse was that he is a man with needs, and since his fiancée was keeping him waiting until their wedding night, he needed an outlet for his needs."

"You mean his fiancée chose to stay a virgin until their wedding night, and he was punishing her for it!?!"

"I—you know what? That is exactly what happened, hah! I never actually thought of it this way before. He always said he would only marry a 'virgin bride' but that rule did not necessarily apply to him!"

"What is his name?"

"Oh, Fadi the jerk, obviously." Danya should have noted the sudden interest in his voice and features, but she was deep in thought.

"What did he tell you after he cheated on you?"

"He came to my house the first time and tried to convince me that it was all my fault, and then he tried saying that it was for my own good that he was sowing his wild oats before marriage, he......." And Danya looked into Devdas's face with shock—and horror. "You—you tricked me!"

He jumped to his feet and went over to her. He was angrier than she had ever seen him before. "I tricked you? You are a natural liar, obviously. So, you were engaged before and did not see the need to tell me?"

Danya was stunned that he would be so mad. She swallowed a lump in her throat and tried to answer calmly, or at least reasonably, "But Devdas, you never asked me about my life before today!"

"Well, I did not think there was this much going on in your life to ask about. I thought you were just Zaara's oh-so-innocent friend."

That made her spring to her feet with anger, too. Facing him, she was still trying to stay calm, and not yell with the injustice of it all. "I would have thought this would make you even happier, one more negative thing about me to throw in your family's face." He started pacing. "Happy that my wife was engaged to another man? Do you know how sacred an engagement is in my country?"

"And in my country, also. But guess what? Marrying somebody to punish your ex and your family does not do much for 'sacred' either. At least I did not wait until I was married and then try and fix the mistake or run away from it. I realized that it would not have worked at the right time—sort of." She added the last two words guiltily in an undertone, but Devdas heard her, and he asked a bit more calmly. "How long ago were you engaged?"

She shifted away from Devdas, feeling discomfort pushing next to her anger, "I was engaged for six months— but I had known Fadi for almost five years. It only took me that long to figure out we were not meant to be!"

"When did you break off your engagement?"

"Umm... two days before I came here to India."

"What?!?" He backed away from her, but he was not yelling anymore, he was just trying to understand. "So you barely lost one guy and already set your eyes on another! You did not waste any time, did you?"

Now pride tears were stinging her eyes, but she refused to look away, or attempt to wipe her face. "It was not like that—you make it all sound so cheap and terrible."

"Then explain more to me." Sitting back in his chair and folding his arms, while staring at her as if he had never seen her properly before, he motioned for her to start talking.

"Listen Devdas, what I did that day is my business and mine alone, well, and Fadi's, but it has nothing to do with you—and if you are implying that I had planned for all of this to happen, you are very mistaken."

"You keep saying 'that day', what day are you talking about exactly?"

Danya sighed, wiping her face quickly with the back of her hand, and realizing that Devdas was not going to let the subject go, she sat down again and spoke in a calm voice that was shaking slightly, "I ran out on my wedding—literally. I was walking down the aisle, and then I was running away, like a bad scene from a movie. It was not the smartest move, I should not have waited until the actual wedding day to run off, I should have run much sooner. I had to only look into Fadi's face to realize that there was no love lost between us, somebody once told me that we had the type of personalities that we only bring out the worst in each other, and it could not have been any more clear than on that day, but for the longest time Fadi had taken me for granted, that even I got used to it. That day, I broke free. I came here two days later, and you know the rest."

Devdas sat in silence just staring at her, appraising, then quietly asked. "Why did you marry me? I never actually asked you for a real answer before; I only accepted what you had told me when we first got married."

Now she had to avert her eyes from his. "I told you. I needed to run away from my life, I have been living in America for almost fifteen years, it is a beautiful country, with so many great things going on for most people, I just never had that sense of belonging there, and the problem is that I do not have a sense of belonging in Jordan anymore either, so that was that. I do watch a lot of Hindi movies, and you know how most of them have happy endings, and then the sign drops 'The End', clearly I did not think there would be more after that sign in real life, that reality sets in, and of course there is a motive to why you wanted to marry me out of the blue."

Danya looked away from him, hurt again by that admittance, and wishing with all her heart that she could tell him how much she really loved him—but opted out.

Instead she said with a sad smile, "I should have realized you were going to make me pay for puking all over you the first time we met."

He burst out laughing, clearly surprised with her odd sense of humor, and made a face. "Don't remind me—I cannot look at laddus anymore."

And that made her laugh too. *If only!*

"Yeah, sorry about that, but you can always have some of my kaju rolls. I can share."

Going down the stairs to have dinner later on that day, Devdas held out his hand and took hers gently in his. She asked him for something. "I want to go a temple, please."

Devdas did not ask why, and early next morning he drove Danya to a nearby temple where she gave her offerings in thanks for his recovery, and received blessings that she did not yet under-stand, but that made her feel at peace with herself and the world.

Afterwards, Devdas took her out to lunch, they bought some new dresses for her, and they did some Sight-seeing. Returning home that night, Danya's heart was filled with newfound hope that maybe, just maybe.

Sitting alone in her room that night, and thinking about how wonderful Devdas was, Danya's thoughts drifted to the last time Fadi had cheated on her, he came to her house to 'reason' with her, as he had done before, he did not count on her being wiser this time around. "If it had been the other way around Fadi, you would have left me a long time ago. I want you out of my house this instant. Don't you dare come near me ever again—it is really over between us." Danya was walking towards the front door to let him out, but he grabbed her arm and turned her towards him. With the saddest look on his face, he was pleading with her to take him back, when she tried to pull herself away from him, and started yelling at him to leave her alone, he actually slapped her! After getting over her shock, Danya tried again to get him out of her house, but he was pleading now, telling her that she had pushed him into all of it, and he cried. And like a fool, Danya took him back. From that day on, she had no love and no respect left in her for him. And not much respect for herself. She was still hesitant to leave even then! She never told anybody about that incident, not even Zaara, for she was always against women staying with men who abused them, and yet she was still holding on to her relationship with Fadi. For the first couple of years after they met, Fadi was the most loving and attentive person she had ever met in her life. Not that Danya had ever had a real relationship before, just a normal crush once or twice, and the one time she thought she was in love she was real young and Tareq was a Muslim, so it was doomed from the beginning. He still held a special place in her heart to this day, just because he was a gentleman. And then she met Fadi. After the second year things started going downhill—at first it was small things, like him trying to imply she was not smart enough on several occasions, especially in front of people, and then she was not good looking enough. Putting Danya down was becoming more of a habit to Fadi. By their third year together, he did not bother with kindness anymore, unless he needed her to do something for him. She was riding an emotional roller coaster by then, was always exhausted, confused and pretty much drained. But by their fourth year together, she found herself just taking it, working more on her studies, and her writing, and she was ignoring Fadi's mood swings more. She learned to just live with it. Danya knew she was a creature of habit, change scared her—so she mostly stuck with what she had in her life, no matter how unhappy it was making her, as long as she did not have to deal with starting anything new, she escaped into her imaginary world. It was always like that—when they started to hang out with other couples, Fadi would either ignore her completely, sometimes even forgetting to introduce her to new people, or worse, he would start putting her down and making jokes at her expense. When Danya tried to explain to him how it was all hurting her and hurting their relationship, or what was left of it even, he started turning it around and telling her it was all in her head, her 'wild imagination' as he called it, that she was becoming too sensitive. Danya stopped going out with him when other people were included. When they had a fight, he would either turn on her and tell her to her face that she was becoming delusional, or he would start making new promises to change—promises that would never last more than the day they were made. And if she got mad, he wondered why she was short tempered. *How do you push somebody to the edge and wonder why they are losing their temper or even their mind? How do people play mind games and try and mess with another human being's psyche and then accuse the other person of being on the verge of a mental breakdown? Is it a game for those people to see how far they could push before they break that human being?* But through it all she still loved Fadi, somehow, but she did not like him anymore—between him and Rose, his mother, she was sure she would eventually lose her mind. Rose was no better, she enjoyed making Danya miserable whenever they met, because clearly nothing and nobody was good enough for her precious son—in her eyes, even Danya herself was not. Rose never let go of an opportunity to tell Danya how great all the other girls she met throughout her life were—and how her precious son could have done better! Danya had to hold her tongue a thousand times from telling her to, by all means, go find her son a better 'victim'. At first Danya used to argue with Fadi about his mother trying to run their life, but he always took Rose's side, no matter how wrong and disrespectful she would be, but even trying to stand up for herself started to wear her down. She did not want to spend any more of her time or energy expecting Fadi to have a sense of understanding or justice. Danya started to just let things go—no matter how hurtful they were—she just was running out of self-esteem, and it was building up on the inside: pure anger, rage and hatred, for Fadi, his mother....and for herself. Coming back to the present, she thought. *When do you actually realize that your relationship is worthless? That all the love you give and expect is worthless? That you eventually become worthless in a miserable relationship? How far are you willing to go before you throw in the towel and just get the hell out? How do you not crack under so much emotional and mental pressure? How far could your turning a blind eye to your own misery take you?* She put it all on paper and pondered over it for a moment. And then gave a sigh of relief. *That was then, now my life is in my own hands... almost.*

The next morning she was going down to the kitchen when she heard Mrs. Khanna and Zohar getting ready to leave. "We will be at my sister's place all day. Poonam is taking the day off today also, could you and Dev manage with dinner?" Mrs. Khanna wondered.

"Sure. Have a good time, and please give Pooja aunty my regards."

It was actually a great opportunity for Danya to go

about the house. She prepared some middle- eastern food, hoping Devdas would not mind that it was not as spicy as Indian food, and they were sitting down for a quiet early dinner, alone for once.

"You are a good cook. I have never tried middle-eastern food before. This is very good."

"Thank you, I am glad you like it." She smiled happily and proudly.

After dinner they went out to the garden to have their tea, and again Devdas was showing interest in her views and writing. "I just finished reading two of your books. They are quite good, I don't read romance usually, so I'm not the best judge out there, but since you told me you write, I ordered the books. They are good, but I think your new one is better, it is more about your thoughts and beliefs than your dreams." She turned a deep shade of crimson... if only he really knew about her dreams nowadays. "Did Fadi support you working, or was it hard for him not having you around a lot of the time?"

With a somewhat sad and sarcastic smile Danya said, "Believe it or not, Fadi never showed any interest in my work, whether when I painted, and not when I started writing and selling books. He is one of those people who do not care about things that do not affect them personally."

"You know what's amazing about you Danya? You do live in your own little world a bit too much, it is a good thing, don't get me wrong, but you have to understand this world we live in to survive it. To most people life is a game, how well you play is what gets you ahead of everybody else."

"That, I never understood. I understand that liars believe no one, and thieves trust no one, but to step on other human beings—literally—to get to higher places or for monetary gains, is something I do not understand. Honestly, I hope I never do."

"This is true of a lot of people, unfortunately, but if you live with your head in the clouds, how do you watch your step? You have to be a good liar, to believe your own lies, for people to believe them, also. That's how you get lied to so easily, and that's why you find it hard to understand people, what you say is what you really mean, and not everybody on this planet is that way. You have to be able to distinguish between genuine people and those who pretty much lie for a living."

"What you are saying is that Fadi, for instance, believed all his lies and thus sold them to me?"

"Absolutely."

Danya leaned back in her chair, with a sick feeling in her stomach, letting out a faint "Wow." Devdas smiled at her with amazement. "You know, you are one in a million—if that." And he went inside the house without saying another word. After it took Danya two whole minutes to get over her shock of being kind of praised by Devdas, she realized one thing: true, she might be dim as to how the world works, but she did notice that Devdas always left her sight after saying anything nice about her—in a way. *Could I Hope!* She shook her head and laughed at her own foolishness. *I never learn: optimism could come in overdose.*

Zaara came home on Tuesday, and as soon as she and Rohan got settled in, she called Danya to let her know she was coming to visit and congratulate her and Devdas on Thursday. Danya was very excited to see her friend again, but did not know how to tell Devdas. *How would he react to hearing Zaara's name and seeing her in person again?* Danya decided not to say anything to him, she would just have to wait and see.

On Wednesday, Danya decided to go the extra mile, since Devdas had stopped attempting to use her as a punishment to his mother! She pulled her hair up, put on some makeup and she put on a new sari. In all her time in India she was wearing regular clothes, but on this day she wanted to do something for herself, she could not believe she had been in India for almost a month. It felt much longer, and yet shorter, for so much had happened in such a short time. Within four weeks she went from almost getting married to one man, to being married to the man of her dreams, as cliché as that might be. The olive green and gold silk sari she was wearing complimented her fair skin, and highlighted her green eyes. She knew she looked pretty, and was very excited as she rushed downstairs to meet her husband at the door. She was waiting by the front door, and as soon as she heard his car pulling in front of the house, she opened the big oak doors and walked outside with a brilliant, welcoming smile. The smile froze on her face when she saw Devdas's expression.

"What do you think you're doing?" He pretty much growled.

"I thought you would like it, you know. I am trying to fit in."

"I don't want you to fit in, I already told you to just be yourself."

"But..."

"No buts—just go back inside, and put on one of the new dresses we bought the other day. You need to stop trying to pretend you're something that you are not. Just be yourself for a change!"

Danya was standing very still, not sure whether that was a confirmation that he liked and accepted her the way she was, or he was still trying to do the ridiculous punishment thing! She had a bad feeling it was the latter. Maybe news of Zaara's return had reached him. She took a steadying breath, and said with calm that she did not feel on the inside—a storm was brewing in her heart, and stomach. Her voice was controlled, but her hands were shaking badly as she stood her ground.

"I am tired of playing your games Devdas. Do you really think you are punishing Zaara this way? She is married; she moved on, she actually loves Rohan. Ma*ji* and Zohar do not necessarily love me, but they accept me as your wife, and from what I understand from Zohar, your whole family does, except for you. The only person who is being punished here is me—nobody else cares that you married an Arab-American Christian anymore, they all moved on except for you—and me."

Turning and going up to her room as fast as she could, Danya was too hurt to even cry, and she was beyond frustrated: mentally tired and emotionally exhausted. *Enough is enough!* She was changing into jeans and a t-shirt. When she heard the front door being opened, and many cheerful hellos and namastes being exchanged, she figured it must be one more family member that she had to face and put up with more disapproving looks to please her husband. She was going down the stairs, when she heard Devdas talking in the small drawing room, where he always received his friends. Her hand was on the door knob, readying herself for more scrutiny, when Devdas's voice reached her ears. He sounded upset, and she was not ready yet to deal with more frustrations and upset, so she was thinking of backing away, when she realized that her husband was actually talking to Zaara!

"Have you lost your mind Dev? You really think it is an option for me to leave my husband, whom I Love and you leave your wife who by the way is my best friend?!?"

"I still don't understand why you refused to elope with me in America when I came for you."

"I cannot believe we are even having this conversation! You are married to Danya, whom I supposed you loved, I am married to Rohan, and I do love him."

"Prove it."

"What?"

"Prove to me that it is over between us once and for all, that you don't love me. I will not let you go this time until you prove to me that this is it."

"You must have lost your mind to be acting like a lovesick teenager! I'm leaving Dev. When you do come to your senses, please do tell Danya that I stopped in today to see her because I missed her, and for her sake I will pretend this conversation never happened." And there was a scuffling noise. Danya peaked around the door in time to see them kissing—or to be exact, Devdas kissing Zaara like his every breath needed hers. Danya was backing away, not wanting to be seen, but her sobs were louder than an explosion. She ran up to her bedroom, Devdas and Zaara on her heels. When they got to her bedroom Danya stopped by the window to catch her breath. With closed eyes she willed herself to calm down. She could feel them behind her. Trying to reach out for her, Devdas said carefully.

"I am sorry Danya—we were trying to resolve an old issue, and things got out of my hands in there. But really... nothing happened, I was just........."

Danya did not turn around to face them, she just could not. She managed to talk with some dignity, although her voice was hoarse and strange to her own ears. "Get out and leave me alone."

Devdas and Zaara exchanged a look, and Zaara was trying to move towards Danya, when she turned around and started yelling, "GET OUT—GET OUT. Both of you... OUT. For once listen to what I want Dev. I WANT YOU TO GET OUT AND LEAVE ME ALONE."

It was her tone that actually scared them, they looked alarmed, and Devdas ashamed, but at that moment Danya did not care. How could she? They betrayed her. He betrayed her. She took a deep breath, wiping away her face and turning her back to them, she said again, calmly but with an edge to her voice. "You need to leave me alone now. There is no more damage to be done to me. Go talk it out with whomever you want. Just leave me alone. Go—both of you, just go. Please."

Danya still had her back turned to them, but she heard the door closing behind her, and that was when she went into action, grabbing her purse, stuffing some of her belongings in a small handbag, she went out quietly and she left through the back door. She heard people talking, but she did not care to stop and listen. She wanted to be as far away as possible. To her amazement, Danya found Devdas's car still parked in front of the house, with his car keys still in there. She put the address for Goa's international airport in the navigation system, and within a couple of minutes was on her way there.

Getting to the airport almost an hour later, everything turned into a blur for Danya. She bought a plane ticket to San Francisco. She thanked the heavens as there was a flight leaving soon, and within three hours was sitting in her seat. She slept the whole way back. As soon as she landed in San Francisco it finally got to her—she might never see Devdas again. *How and why would I go back when he did not want me in the first place? How could he do this to me after we had all the talks about cheating spouses and partners?*

She managed to get out of the airport, get a taxi and make it home without acting crazy in front of strangers—and she found the spare key that Blake had left her inside a safe box outside, she was in control, but as soon as she was inside her house, she was dragging herself to make it to the kitchen. Crying and sobbing like a lost child, she made herself a cup of hot herbal tea, took a couple of aspirins and then fell asleep on the sofa in front of the television. Thankfully, she did not dream, for as soon as she opened her eyes, it hit her all over again. *This is not going to work—I have to get out of here—I will regain control over my life, somehow.*

It actually took her the whole morning to get off the couch, and out of the house. She was in desperate need for fresh air. Danya was walking aimlessly, when she started suspecting she might actually be going mad—her feet had lead her to the park where Devdas used to meet Zaara! She sat near the fountain, just waiting—and looking into every man's face, to see if she could find Devdas. She dipped her hand in the water, and blessed herself. *Crazy—pagal—crazy.* Words just kept going through her mind. *Pathetic... how could I have been so pathetic to actually think that he likes me, let alone that he would one day love me? That we might have had a real future together beyond the past? How could I have been so blind! There has to be something wrong with me, first Fadi and now Devdas! People might wonder if I enjoy tormenting myself on purpose...but no... no pain I endured with Fadi during those five miserable years was ever as bad as those five seconds. He never even seemed interested in touching me at all, while I'm supposedly his wife and then he goes kissing somebody else's wife!*

She was praying for just a glimpse of his face—and then praying she would never be put to the test...what would she have done had she seen him? Throw herself into his un-wanting arms? Or yell at him for not realizing how much love he was throwing away? Love he never asked for to begin with? Danya's biggest fear was that one day they would meet, and Devdas might not even recognize her. That night, she had a nightmare: she was lost, and running up to Devdas, but he had a blank look on his face, like he'd never seen her before in his life—and he kept walking away and Danya just standing there, trying not to choke on her tears. She woke up from her sleep to a strange strangled noise, and it took her a couple of seconds to realize the wounded animal sounds were coming from her own throat—she was choking on her own breath. *How can I love Devdas so much, when he caused me so much hurt, and not break in half?* She did not seem able to pull herself together, it was like part of her soul was wrenched away from her.

Eight
Humko Tumse Pyaar Hai (I love only you!)

"She loves you Dev. She is in love with you. More than I ever was, and more than anybody else on earth possibly ever would." Zaara and Devdas were at the airport, it had only taken them nearly the whole day to realize where Danya had disappeared to. Getting to the airport fast, they bought Devdas a ticket on the next flight out, and were waiting for his flight.

"She can't be. You don't understand, I did not exactly make her life easy during the past three weeks—I was brooding, and acting like a teenager with no self-control. I took my anger at my mother and you out on her, and she took it pretty well, kind of."

"Because she loves you, and she sees no fault in anything

you do. I am sure she loves you still—and I know you love her."

Shaking his head before covering his face with his hands, Devdas let out a deep sigh. "I do—I really do. I'm not sure how or even when... not sure of much right now, but I do love Danya." Then turning to Zaara with an amused smile, he added, "Isn't it amazing that we are having this conversation—you and I?"

Zaara smiled back, and said. "Dev, we loved each other when we were pretty much children, we did not see each other or even talk to each other properly for almost three years. I think we got used to the idea that we were in love with each other that we forgot that we really do not know each other anymore. It's only sad that Danya had to get hurt before you realized the truth." And then she laughed, adding, "Do you realize that she was always so worried about you? She thought that you might one day turn into the character from 'Devdas' the movie!"

Laughing also at his wife's simplicity, Devdas looked at Zaara and said, "Will you ever forgive me my childishness? I know I've been acting ridiculously for the past two months, if not more, my anger at losing you made me act like a person I never thought I could be. To say I was wrong would be too kind, but I do really like for us to remain friends, and I hope one day you will have it in you to forgive me and somehow to forget."

Zaara smiled at him again. "Of course I do forgive you. You have to bring Danya back, that's all that matters now."

"I don't know where she could be; in America or even back in Jordan by now!"

Handing him a piece of paper, Zaara told him, "I have

her address in America written down here for you, and if she's not there, you can get her address in Jordan from Fadi, I wrote his phone number down for you as well. I don't know if Danya kept her same phone number since she lost her phone on her wedding day, but you can give that a try first before calling Fadi."

Devdas looked at the paper with a twisted smile. "That would be a delight, asking Danya's ex where she would be—and if he knows......"

Zaara let out an amused laugh. "Jealous?"

"Crazy jealous is more like it! It burns me on the inside to think of her with another man."

"Good." Devdas raised an eyebrow—Zaara laughed and finished, "I mean it's good to see you showing your love for her, for a change."

"Do you think that she will come back with me?" He sounded very unsure of himself.

"I pray to the Gods that she does." Zaara replied kindly.

"I will call you when I get there and meet her, pray for us."

"I will. I have to leave. Rohan must be outside by now."

"I never asked you, does he know about us?"

"Yes, it was one of the first things I told him before we got married, when they were still discussing our marriage actually, and his response was that he realizes that I am a human being with feelings of my own, and having been in love before marriage did not make me less than the person he always wished to be his wife, me. This is what made me appreciate, respect and love him even more."

"He is a great man, much greater than I could have ever been. Please give him my regards—and Zaara, thank you for everything." After shaking hands, each of them was on his way.

The doorbell was ringing in the early morning, Danya got out of bed, made sure her t-shirt and pants were suitable to see who was calling on her so early in the morning. She looked at the hall clock, eight thirty! *Maybe it's the mailman.*

It was Fadi. After the awkward hellos, Danya let him in.

"I have been coming to your house every day, in the hopes of finding you here." Fadi said to her as she led him to the living room and stood facing him with a weary and tired face.

"Why?" She couldn't help sounding rude... and defeated.

"What do you mean why?"

"Why do you want to see me, what is there left to be said Fadi?"

"I wanted to talk to you. When you left, you did not give me a chance to say anything."

"There was nothing left to be said between us. You broke so many beautiful feelings inside of me. I was dragging myself through an unhappy, unhealthy relationship. Don't tell me you felt miserable beyond the first five minutes, I know relief when I see it, I have felt it, too."

Fadi sat quietly on a chair, just watching Danya, realizing he never looked at her, really looked at her, for the longest time since they had first met, and then he asked her. "I heard from the people at the coffee house that after you went to India with Zaara, and going back and forth, one of Zaara's acquaintances here told me that her American friend had accompanied her to India, and had married Zaara's ex-boyfriend. Is that true?"

"Yes... I got married to Zaara's ex, Devdas, about three weeks ago."

His eyes widened with shock even though he already knew about her marriage. And he wondered, "Do you love him?" And he then added, not unkindly, "What brings you back here then?"

"Fadi, I am here because I don't know where else to go. I know I don't plan on staying here. I loved Devdas probably from the first moment I laid eyes on him, as farfetched as that looks and sounds right now. When I was with you, you made me lose myself, and my self-respect to the point of hating the person I had become, and I started hating you for it. I came back to settle a couple of matters, and then I will leave. I don't know where to, but I know it needs to be somewhere away from you... and away from Devdas. You both almost killed me, in a sense, and I refuse to be weak ever again: not in love, and not for love. It is just not worth it. You were right about one thing though, I was totally obsessed with Hindi movies that eventually my own life resembled a really bad one."

Fadi flinched, and was looking at her with astonishment mingled with worry. For a while it seemed that he was struggling with words. "I had no idea—I am sorry. I really am Danya. I don't know what else to say. I acted like a complete jerk."

"Oh, Fadi, we are alike in some ways—you always want what you don't have, and as soon as you get it, you shatter it to pieces, and then blame the world for it. Don't get upset with me, I told you, we are somewhat alike in that, I just never realized it at the time until my world shattered. I set myself up for this, every step of the way. You just helped."

"What about Devdas?" He wondered again about her husband.

Danya smiled— more like a wince. Just hearing his name was making her ache all over, like someone hit her in the chest. "Devdas opened my eyes to my faults as well as his. You know, like the fact that there was never any appreciation in our relationship, yours and mine, just the need to ask for more, both you and I did that. Goodness alone was never enough. You are a generous person, very thoughtful with others and even kind, it's just me that you could not bring yourself to share those qualities with and I accept that now. At the end of the day, each of us has to move on—separately for the sake of sanity, or at least for the sake of what's left of mine."

Danya sat down, her legs were shaking... she was shaking all over. She was saying the right words that her brain said were right, but her heart was aching for Devdas all the same. Even after all she had been through, she knew she could never get over Devdas so easily. And in a way it bothered her even more that she did not even bring one picture of him with her, not that she needed it: his face was imprinted on her brain and heart. All she wanted to do was close her eyes, and keep him in front of her, and then she was wishing she would never blink again in her life.

"Are you okay? You look too pale." Fadi got out of his seat and was standing next to her now, looking at her with concern. He knelt in front of her but did not attempt to touch her.

"I feel very hollow—if that is even possible. It feels like my life just ended, but someone forgot to drop 'The End' sign, like I am being dragged through my own life, whether I like it or not. Do I sound too dramatic to you Fadi?"

"Actually, you sound like you are in deep shock. You could use a sleeping pill and a long nap. Go ahead, take a nice warm shower, I will make you some herbal tea, and grab you a couple of sleeping pills from the corner store."

"Thank you. I don't need pills, I don't take pills. The tea does sound good, I will make it though." She was getting out of her seat, but Fadi sat her back down gently. He placed a pillow behind her back, and kissed the top of her head like he was kissing a child.

"Please, I want to do this for you. Let me take care of you, even if it's for a little while, and then I will leave you alone."

With her eyes closed, Danya's life was flashing by like a lousy movie that is too long, and bores to death. Unshed tears were stinging her eyes, but she refused to let go.

Five minutes later Fadi was sitting down with his own cup of tea, after finishing hers she sat back in the chair again, and looked at him. She really had no feelings left for him in her, just a memory of the friendship they once shared before it all went downhill.

Seeing that Danya was calmer, Fadi asked her gently. "I asked you earlier, but you didn't tell me, why are you here?"

"I told you Fadi, I am here because I don't know where else to go. I only know I want to be far away from everything and everybody right now."

"I really am sorry for the way I acted before."

"Oh, you acted like a man. I'm beginning to think that ninety percent of men are just like that."

"No they're not—just the ones you met along the way. You really should have been there for the 'How to pick an engaging and decent husband' day at school."

Danya smiled, and for some horrific reason, her smile turned into sobs—she was crying like she had when she was eighteen, and her parents had just died—just sobbing and spluttering. "I'm—I'm not sure what's wrong with me... I... I don't know..."

Fadi was beside her, and then he was holding her in his arms like he would hold and console a miserable child. "Hush—it's all going to be okay. Everything will be fine."

"Nothing is—nothing is okay. Nothing will ever be fine again, I just don't know what to do with myself anymore."

"Don't talk like that. You know what you want, you always knew. You dreamt of a happy, simple life, a stronger you, and guess what? You don't need me or anybody else for that. You are stronger than you give yourself credit for, you knew we were wrong for each other, and took a step to get out of that situation."

"Yes, I can see how strong I looked running out of that church in my wedding dress." They both gave a shaky laugh. And she finished. "I always wanted to get out of our relationship, but did not have enough courage, or maybe I was afraid of being alone. I had to come to terms with running out on you, only to do it again with Devdas. I'm sorry, I should have said something before—I should have been more decent about it."

"Please don't apologize. I am the one who should do that. The signs were all there that you were miserable, I just did not take the time to look deeper for what was really troubling you, or even look deeper for what made you run off. I had treated you horribly, and I am very sorry for all of it."

"Hey! I guess we are even then." Smiling into his face through her tears, Danya was realizing how right Zaara had been, she did bring out the worst in Fadi just like he brought out the worst in her. "We always were better off as friends. We should just stick to that."

"That sounds just right. Did I tell you, after you left, I went out and bought all your books, and read every single one?" And he added as Danya looked up to him in shock, "I know, about time, too, hah!" He leaned back and told Danya, "Since you left I have not been to my parents' house as much. I did a lot of soul searching after you left, I won't deny that I was very mad at you at first, but then when I calmed down I became more worried than angry. During it all my mother was the least helpful person possible!" Shaking his head sadly, Fadi told Danya that after she left he realized that he actually loved her mostly because she was Arabic, which was what his parents expected of him, to marry an Arabic girl! "I always turned a blind eye to my father's weakness against my mother's treatment of him; and I am sorry to say that I took some of it out on you, as weird as that might sound to you. I watched my father evolving from a doormat to 'wall to wall carpeting' since childhood and that terrified me to death. I am not telling you this to say that I was right in anything I did before. I am just trying to explain my mind set to you, I need you to understand that I have no excuse for having treated you the way I had, but there was something mean inside of me that would just resurface and would not go back in. I hope that you might understand what was going on with me. I am ashamed to say this, but I did take it for granted that no matter what happened, you would always be there. Do you understand what I'm trying to say Danya?"

"Yes I do. That's pretty much what Zaara told me about you and I being at each other's throats all the time. I let you think that because I let go of standing up for myself and turned into what I always disrespected about women and men. I was good about giving lectures on what's wrong with the world, but never even tried to change the things that I could!"

"It must have been great to have me help you lose faith in yourself and humanity! I was in a bad position myself. It finally hit me that my mother *loved* me as a possession more than a son or a human being! When you left, I was hopping mad, and her idea of consoling me was to tell me, while we were still there at church, that I should be thankful because she thought SHE deserved better! And then she suggested I start looking for somebody else! We are still in church! I'm apologizing to everybody and their cousin, and my mother's main concern was how all of that was affecting HER!! And all last month she's been going on and on about how she'd given up her life to her family and expected more from us to make her happy! That's when it hit me; it is always about her! SHE has to be happy with her life—SHE has to be happy with MY life! Nobody else mattered. Certainly not my father, and I just came to realize, not even me! The world has to evolve around her and only her! I'm trying to find out what I want myself, how I feel about all of this, and honestly, how I ever felt about you and me. I really hope one day you could forgive me for at least some of the hurt I caused you."

He was now giving her a friendly hug, announcing the end of their past, and it felt great not to have the anger and hurt anymore.

"Could I have a word with my wife please?"

Danya jumped a mile in shock, and Fadi nearly pushed

her to the ground as he spun around to look into Devdas's face.

"The screen door was open, I knocked, but when nobody came, I let myself in. Danya, I would like to have a word with you."

I must have gone mad—finally! Devdas!! Here!

Danya pulled herself together, still staring into Devdas's face, while Fadi got hold of himself faster than she did, and moved forward, extending a hand to Devdas.

"Hello, you must be Devdas. I'm Fadi Faraj—uh, Danya's friend."

Devdas raised an eyebrow, yet shook hands with Fadi, and they both turned to look at Danya, who was still standing with eyes wide open with shock. Devdas's face held no expression, as he said, "Danya. Can we talk?"

Fadi looked about for a second, and then said. "I should go. I have a meeting in ten minutes. I hope to see you both soon." He shook hands with Devdas again, did not dare go near Danya, but gave her a reassuring smile as he practically ran out the door.

"What are you doing here, Dev?" Danya finally found her voice.

Noting that she only called him 'Dev' when she was upset, Devdas sat down in the chair that Fadi had occupied a while ago. Danya, on the other hand, was moving away from him, she just did not trust herself being that close to him, and not yearn for him—her pathetic heart does not learn! He looked uncertain for a moment, looking around the room, and then cleared his throat.

"I got your address from Zaara, who by the way sends you her love. I came here to see you because there is so much to clear between us."

"We don't have much to talk about. I don't want anything from you, only my freedom." Shock and hurt were making her stronger, and in a way cruel. He was looking surprised to hear her tone, and the words, but still sat down and waited for her to calm down. Instead every moment made her more tense and her heart ache. *How can I love somebody so much that it hurts to breathe without him? Not fair.* And she did not intend to be fair at that moment. "Really Dev, what else do you want from me?"

"You."

"What?" It was almost a whisper.

"I want you." He answered simply. She turned on him furiously and almost shouted.

"Is this some kind of a sick joke? Or do you still think this sham of a marriage is actually bothering anybody else but me? Zaara moved on, sorry to break the news to you. They might not love me, but our marriage is no punishment to your mother or Zohar. The only person who was humiliated, hurt and mentally abused was me. No more. Find somebody else, or some other way to get even with all of them, I'm done. This is just not worth it. You really thought you could come here and say a couple of words, and that it would solve everything? Why you married me, that you kissed my married friend while you yourself are still married to me? What if you had walked in right now and saw me and Fadi kissing! How would that have made you feel?"

"It would have ripped my heart out, because I love you Danya." Devdas said it so gently, Danya almost missed it—and then looked as if she had been punched in the face.

"Another lie Dev? Please do not use the word love, you do not love, you get obsessed with the idea of love, first it was Zaara—and now it's my turn! Exactly for how long are you going to 'love' me Devdas?"

"What do you mean?"

"Simple. How long are you going to love me? Till you're sure how ridiculous this whole thing was and is? Or till I fall in love with you again and then you're bored and need to move on to another obsession? No thank you. I am done Dev."

"Love me again?" He wondered in a whisper. Danya was just realizing she had said too much, and tried to retract, but Devdas had got to his feet, and approached her carefully, as if he was afraid that she might run again. He was so close, and yet—she badly wanted to believe in what he said. He was standing so close now, she could almost feel his breath on her skin, and it made her whole body want to lean into his. She did not dare look into his eyes— until he lifted her face up gently to look into her eyes. "Fall in love with me again? Do you not love me anymore?"

"I—I might have loved you—but—but not..." She really could not bring herself to look into those gorgeous eyes and deny loving him still. She loves him beyond reason. "I... Devdas, I..."

He then bent down and kissed her full on the lips—and the rest was history. She was taking in his every breath, kissing him with hunger she did not know she possessed, with every heartbeat telling him she loves him, and he said he loved her! Her love for him is more than her love for life itself, and being near him again would be enough. *If it's true he could let go of Zaara.*

Danya pulled her lips away from his, but was still holding on to him with her hands on his chest, feeling his heartbeat going crazy under her palms. She did not trust her shaking legs to hold her up if she let go. "I can't do this—I cannot do this anymore, Devdas."

"What exactly can't you do?" His voice was hoarse... deep and so warm on her face.

"This, these games that you like to play. I can't be part of them anymore. I can't be your mother's punishment, or Zaara's. I want to be wanted for my own being. I want my husband's love, not punishment for something that I had no hand in. I want..."

The rest of her words were lost in another gentle kiss, and now she could feel his hunger for her, too, he was whispering near her mouth. "I am sorry— sorry for kissing Zaara to prove a childish point, sorry for the pain I caused you, for the misunderstandings, sorry for all of it. I wish if you could forgive me, I want you to love me always. I don't know how I can ever live without you in my arms again. I will spend every waking moment of my life making it up to you, all the pain I caused you. I love you Danya, I love you and I cannot remember what life was before being with you, and I cannot imagine how it would be like without you. You have been gone but a day, and I felt more lost and miserable than I had ever felt before in my life. Realizing that I was in love with you to the point where I could not remember Zaara or the ridiculous reason we got married for, that made me more nervous and scared than I had ever been in my entire life, and made me act like a fool when Zaara came over. I am not asking you to come with me right away, we could try and get to know each other more. We have been in India, you know my life there, I would like to know more about your life here, and then we will see if it would suit you to come back home with me."

Home! Such a wonderful word, and now it was Danya's

turn to stand on her tiptoes and kiss her husband. She was holding on to him as if she was holding onto dear life.

"I love you Devdas—I love you so very much. I always did, and I always will."

Later on that day, Danya called Zaara, who gushed, "I'm so glad it all worked out well between the two of you. You know I would never do anything to hurt you, Danya, or hurt our friendship. Rohan sends you both his love and good wishes. You have to come over as soon as you come back."

"Thank you for everything Zaara. We are working on some issues, and I need to settle matters here before I do anything this time, but I do pray it all works out for the best."

Devdas stayed with Danya for two weeks, occupying the guest room, giving her all the time and space she needed, and she saw a lot more of what she loved about him. There was no pretending with Devdas, as the saying goes: what you see is what you get. He did not try to push her, just let her take her own time with their relationship. Even Blake liked him, when they all met to set her affairs in order. The rest of the time they spent talking, sightseeing, and enjoying getting to know each other all over again. Devdas's interest in her views as a human being, not just a woman, elevated her respect for him tenfold.

They were getting ready to go to a new Indian restaurant that luckily served no dessert, when Devdas received a phone call from Zohar. "I better take this." He said with a frown.

Danya went back into her bedroom to get her jacket, and to give him more privacy. She also got him a jacket, and was admiring for the millionth time how organized and neat everything about Devdas was. The guest room was immaculate. And then he called out for her. "Danya, can you come here, please."

She walked back into the living room, instantly realizing something was very wrong.

"What's the matter?" She put the jackets down and went up to him.

"It's my mother, she is very ill. Zohar just told me that they will have to have an open heart surgery done by tomorrow night at the most, I have to be there." He held her hands in his—and she looked into his beautiful eyes, and actually saw herself in there.

"I have to leave right now to be able to make it on time. I have no idea when I would be able to come back. I love you Danya. I don't promise you an easy life with me in India. We still have a lot to work through, whether it's our religious differences, or the new culture you would have to get used to, but what I do promise that I am going to try my best with you and for you. If you decide you do want to start a new life with me, all you have to do is call me, and I will come back to get you."

The look of doubt and sincerity on his face told Danya without words the depth of his love. And she was sure like never before. "There will be no need to call you."

"Aaah!" He looked startled, and hurt, and Danya laughed in his face, as she bent down touching the hem of his pants like she's seen so many Indian wives do.

"I am coming home with you tonight." And her husband finally let out a glorious laugh, and put his hand on her head, and she got his blessings. And when he pulled her up and into his arms, Danya knew—she was finally home.

The beginning

Nine

Twins

India, 2006

'*L*etting go of life is not as hard as letting go of Devdas, it's like cutting off my arms and legs—like cutting off my lungs! It makes me feel even more helpless, I never imagined that I could ever love someone to where I cannot breathe without him. It's not even something that I had dreamt of for one of my books! Believe me, it took even me by surprise how much love I could hold for one person: more than myself, more than my life, even more than my own children! I hope one day you will have your share of love, if you have not already found it. I used to scoff at people when they say they married their best friend, but I did. Devdas is the best friend anybody could wish for, I shared my thoughts, dreams and life with him, never fearing being misunderstood or judged, he accepted me just the way I am. Devdas would have taken on the world for me had I needed him to—he would stand up for me and take care of me and keep me safe from the world if I needed him to. What do I care about the rest of the world when I had Devdas next to me, with me? I have learned a long time ago that I should never need anybody else to stand up for me, I can take care of my own self, but it is a great feeling to know that the man I am in love with has my back always, no matter what. It's not possible for me to ever put in words how much I love him—but I do, I love him more than I love myself, and I want him to be happy—I want him to be safe—I want him to be able to live when I am not able to be with him anymore. I am blessed to have spent the last four years of my life with such a special human being. I know you're wondering why I left all my belongings to you—I always thought that if things were not the way they are, you should have been entitled to your share of my parents' fortune, and I want to make sure you get your share, now that you can't refuse it—I know your pride, I have it too. I wish we had been a proper family, but wishing to change the past never helped anybody. I would love for you to come and visit my family here. India has to be the most beautiful place on earth... I know what you're going to say: Jordan is beautiful also—I agree, but you still have to see it here. Please take care of my children if you can, and most importantly of Devdas, watch over him for me, he is the best thing that had ever happened to me. You are free to share this letter with him and with my friend Zaara, tell her for me that I am sorry I couldn't tell her about you, and I hope she can forgive me one last time. I hope—I wish for the best for all of you

   Sincerely yours, Danya.'

Devdas read the letter again, his hand was shaking, and

his vision was blurry, but nothing could have ever prepared him for the feeling of emptiness that filled his heart.

"I'm sorry I have startled you—I did not know if Danya had ever mentioned that she has a cousin... a twin sister." He heard the words murmured softly, and he looked up.

The young woman sitting in front of him was looking very uncomfortable, as if not sure what she should be doing or saying. She laced her fingers in her lap, and waited patiently for Devdas to get over his initial shock at seeing her. She probably should have called instead of just showing up at his door step, considering....

Devdas wiped his face, and looked up at Dara, and pain pulled at his heart strings, draining it even more. Three weeks—Danya had died three weeks ago, and never in the past four years had she mentioned having a sister, an identical twin! Clearing his throat, he answered her. "No, she didn't. And her friend Zaara did not know either or she would have told me, and we would have notified you of Danya's... of Danya passing away."

"It was Blake who called me. He's the one who was responsible for Danya's will—I came here because she left everything to me, and I would like in turn to give it to her children. I don't want the money, and it should have been yours and theirs to begin with."

Devdas was shaking his head, still trying to get over his shock, and trying not to show his despair to a person who looked like his beloved, but was for sure not her.

"I don't need the money, I could accept some of it for the children, but Danya was very clear, if she put it in her will that she wanted you to have it, then that's what should be done." He then asked, "If you don't mind me asking, how and why weren't you a part of Danya's life? I mean you are clearly twins, and obviously have not been in touch if she knew nothing about what's going on with your life. She clearly knew where she could find you, though. I have been married to Danya for four years, and I have never heard her mention you, she always said she had no family left after her parents died in the car accident."

Putting her tea cup down on the coffee table, Dara sat back in her chair to look at Devdas more clearly, her voice was clear and carried no emotions as she answered him.

"It all happened so long ago, neither one of us actually remembers that we are sisters. When my birth mother got pregnant, they were overjoyed, but on the same day that she found out she was having twins, her brother broke the news to her that he and his wife could not have children he had a medical condition that could not enable them to have children ever. That's when my birth mother and father decided to give one of their twins to her brother, since the doctors had assured her that the babies were not identical. We were born, and I was legally Radi and Suhair's daughter, and my birth parents kept Danya. For the first seven years we all were inseparable, but then on our seventh birthday, Kal, my birth father, decided that since we looked like identical twins, we should be brought up by him and Nadia, his wife. Of course my parents refused to give me up, I mean, I had been with them for seven years, I only knew that they were my parents, and Nadia and Kal were my aunt and uncle! There were some legal battles, and my birth parents lost the case, especially when I told the judge that I wanted to live with my parents. To make a long story short, we never even saw each other afterwards, and later after they had moved to America, Danya wrote to me a couple of times, especially after her parents passed away, but I was busy with my own parents then, they passed away within a year of each other from cancer, and afterwards I never thought about trying to go see Danya or contacting her. You would have thought that losing our parents would have brought us together, but it did not."

Devdas was looking at her with a mixture of shock, pity, and lots of confusion. "I am sorry about your parents, both birth and adoptive. It must have been hard on you to deal with all of that at such a young age."

"You know, believe it or not, it did not bother me that they gave me away, what bothered me was when they decided they wanted to take me back. They were so selfless that they gave a child away to make their relatives happy, but selfish enough to never stop and think about my feelings, that after living with my adoptive parents for seven years, taking me away from them would have disrupted my life and affected me emotionally and mentally. They had given me the most loving and giving parents in the world, and all of a sudden they wanted to take that away from me. They were right to give me to my parents, and had they not tried to take me back, things would have been very different for me and Danya, we could have been like normal cousins. We were not even normal strangers." She looked at Devdas, not sure how to ask him, but then said, "What went wrong?"

"It all happened so fast, both of her pregnancies were hard, but this last one was very hard on her health, when she delivered Zohra, she developed an infection and had to stay in the hospital, she..." And for the second time, Dara saw his composure crack, he looked lost for words for a minute, then with a choked voice said, "I'm sorry. It was so sudden, I mean, one minute the doctor was telling us the infection was under control and she might leave the hospital within two days, and then he comes out into the lobby to tell us she's gone...just like that!" *And I did not even get to say goodbye.* It was eating at his peace every moment of every day.

Devdas got quiet, and looking out of the window, he was staring unseeingly at the garden—Danya loved the gardens, they had spent so many nights just wandering around, enjoying each other's company. During the last four years he had realized that loving her was an addiction: that was Danya's word, she had teased him once that she was addicted to him. He could still hear her laugh, if he closed his eyes he could pretend it's all a nightmare, and that this is Danya sitting in front of him, enjoying some weird joke. But looking back at Dara, and looking into her eyes—he knew Danya could never take the look of her love for him out of her eyes like that. Even when they argued, she still could not get herself to be angry with him for too long. She once said that all she had to do was look at him, and all her anger would evaporate. He missed her to the point that it was physically painful.

Dara was waiting for him patiently, letting him take his time with his thoughts, and she was seeing his pain... real pain that she never thought would be so touchable, so visible without words.

"Danya, may she rest in peace, never told me anything about her life in Jordan, we talked about everything, from politics to religion to traditions and everyday things—but not once about how she grew up in Jordan."

Sitting back in his chair and looking out of the large windows again, another sadness engulfed Devdas once more—maybe he did not know his wife so well after all, but realizing this did not make the pain of losing her lessen, if possible it made it worse... there was still so much they could have shared. Dara watched him as she was relaxing herself. He obviously loved Danya, and was upset to have lost her so soon, and she could not be angry with Danya for never telling Devdas about her, they had been forced into that strange situation since childhood, and continued to live as strangers even after their parents had passed away. She could have tried to better their relationship but by then each of them had her own life, and got used to not relate to each other. It was too late to blame herself, Danya or any of their parents now. Now was the time to make better choices—she had chosen to be alone in her life for good reasons, never tied down by a husband or a child, people might consider it a form of selfishness, but Dara figured, this was one selfishness that never hurt anybody, and affected no one but herself. Radi and Suhair had tried to find their daughter a suitable husband, but in the end they understood and accepted her point of view and respected her choice. After dealing with their death, Dara never wanted to be close to another human being ever... she could not handle any more pain and loss, even worse, watching somebody she loves so much suffer and die without being able to do anything for them, except uttering meaningless words of comfort. *You go from: everything is going to be all right and having a somewhat good, even strange sense of humor about it, to disbelief and anger, and it is the anger that drags you through it all. I need to understand why? Why does this happen, and what is the reason of human existence? And then I think that God must have a bigger plan, thank him for everything, and try to get on with my life.* But she was not strong enough to do that again. Now she had a choice to make, give Devdas the money and leave, go back to living by herself and for herself, or does she stay and try and help Devdas with the children for a little while... after all, one of them was a newborn. "What's her name? I mean the baby, I'm sorry I did not catch it earlier."

Coming out of his own trance, Devdas said with a voice strangled with emotion. "Zohra, and our boy is named Arjun, after my father. He is three now. Poor kid, I don't know what to tell him when he keeps asking me when mama is coming back home."

"Do you think it would be a bad thing if I went to see them?"

"I don't know how to explain to a three year old that his mother is no more, and that you are only her look-alike cousin? I want you to meet both of them, don't get me wrong. Do you have any ideas of how to go about it?"

Smiling sadly, Dara shook her head no and said, "None at all!" *It's situations like this that I have been running away from... and here I am, with no clue how to handle a real life situation.* "I'm sorry. I have no idea what to say to you."

"Arjun's with my mother, my sister Zohar got married and moved to England two years ago with her husband. I'll have Riya bring them here, we'll tell Arjun that you are Danya's cousin and we'll go from there. I have to prepare ma*ji* for this also. She was very attached to Danya, she is still not over the shock of losing her." *Neither am I, but going on is not a choice at this point: it's a must.*

"Let's just go to them. Is Zohra home?"

"Yes, she had no complications—it was all Danya."

"I'm sorry." Dara said softly, and Devdas could tell that she really was. As they headed up the stairs towards the children's room, Dara was looking around, oblivious to the house and furnishings, and full of anxiety about meeting the children. When Devdas entered the room, Dara followed quietly, he introduced her to Riya, the children's nanny, as Danya's cousin. His mother was in her own room, and then Devdas held the cutest little boy she had ever seen up in his arms, Dara smiled with all her heart.

"Look who came to visit you Arjun, this is your mama's cousin. Her name is Dara."

Arjun smiled shyly and held his arms out for Dara to hold him. As soon as she felt the child in her arms and he looked up into her eyes with beautiful wide green eyes, a new unknown warm feeling filled her up. She fell in love with the child, the unconditional love that holds you prisoner for life. Kissing him on the forehead, and setting him back down to go back to playing with his blocks, Dara then turned to the baby girl. To say she was smitten was an understatement. She held her gently, and nuzzled her face in the baby's neck, and then started crying silently. She cried for the children, for a sister she never really knew, for the parents she lost, and for Devdas's loss. She felt Devdas's hand patting her on the back and turned to look at him, he was unnerved to find there were real emotions behind the cold exterior Dara had presented so far. She looked like a lost child herself, he wanted to offer her help, but held back. Instead, he smiled kindly, took Zohra and placed her back in her crib. She had not even stirred. She was such a good baby.

"Riya says that my mother is taking a nap right now, if you don't mind waiting to meet her we could go downstairs for a fresh cup of tea, and you can try some of our tea biscuits." He informed her.

It took Dara a while to compose herself, and then when they made it back to the living room and she was settled with an aromatic cup of chai in her hands, she said, "I met Danya's ex fiancé, Fadi, when I was in the states getting Danya's paperwork done—he was very sad to hear about Danya, actually he almost had a heart attack when he first saw me—he also did not know about me. He is married now, her name is Talia, and they invited me out to lunch with them while I was there."

"I'm glad he's doing well, for Danya's sake I guess." He said honestly.

Dara was not sure how to say it properly, without imposing on Devdas and his family. So she said, "I would like to stay and help you with the children for a while, if that is not a problem with you or your family."

Devdas was surprised but also sincere in his answer. "That would be very kind of you, and you would not be imposing at all. You are more than welcome to stay for as long as you wish."

Two days later, they were sitting down for breakfast and Devdas was getting ready to leave for work. He had transferred as much of his work as he could to his home office but had to go into the main office at least twice a week. They had closed the New York office as their business in the India office was doing great by itself. Mrs. Khanna, after getting over the initial shock, decided to have Dara sit on her right, and kept patting her on the hand every now and then while tearing up. "You know, Danya was such a wonderful person—kind and generous. After I fell ill about four years ago, she was with me every day with Zohar, helping me and nursing me back to life. No matter how many times I thanked her, and no matter how many times I praise her, it would never be enough. I am sorry she could not have stayed with us longer, but nobody could change or challenge destiny, our time here was pre-destined when we were born. I'm glad that you are here now—and I hope you consider us your family and to stay with us for as long as you'd like."

Devdas was pretending to wipe his mouth, noticing how uncomfortable Dara was when faced with emotions, but heard her replying with a quiet and calm voice. "You are very kind. I'm happy to be here, and would love to stay and help with the children for as long as it's needed. I really have no obligations to go back to in Jordan at the moment."

Devdas got up, gave his mother a hug and said goodbye to all of them, and then left for the day.

That night Dara could not sleep well, it was well after midnight and she was still tossing and turning when she heard the sound of somebody running past her room, she got up quickly and went to the children's room, expecting someone to be there but the night-light revealed no one aside from the children and Riya in there, and then she heard the footsteps again and she rushed out into the hallway only to bump into Devdas. He was soaked in sweat from head to toe, his hair plastered to his face, but Dara was more concerned with the look on his face, one minute it was pure terror, and the next it turned into cheer joy! And she shivered when he laughed and just held her in a bone crushing hug, and then just as she was wondering what had gotten into him, he pulled back and held her face in his hands. Tears were rolling down Devdas's face, but he was still smiling happily, and Dara's confusion grew—she put her hand gently on his shoulder and patted it, and his eyes just blazed. "Oh, thank god, I had the worst nightmare possible—and it felt so real I was terrified."

Dara tried to pull back from him, but even though his touch was gentle, his hold was firm.

"Uh... Devdas. What was your dream about?" And that's when he let go of her—and backed away. Running his fingers through his hair, he mumbled. "Oh, sorry... so sorry. I know you won't believe this, but... um, for a minute there, for one glorious minute, I thought... I thought that it all had been a horrible nightmare. That Danya was.... that she...." And he broke down, the man was actually shaking with sobs, and Dara did not know what to do to comfort him—then she put her hand on his back and started rubbing it, and it bothered her that one, he mistook her for Danya until he heard her voice and two that she actually enjoyed his touch for that one minute! *I have no right—no right whatsoever to feel this way about Devdas—never!* It took Devdas another minute to get a hold on himself, and then he apologized to Dara. "I really am sorry, I don't know how this could have happened. Please do accept my apologies, and know that this would never happen again." And he went back to his room. It took Dara much longer to get back some control over her emotions, it moved her how much he was broken up about losing his wife, but she knew she had to be careful. *Do not lose your head!* So when morning came, Dara decided to act like nothing had happened, and Devdas followed suit. Later on that day Devdas found her in the children's room reading to Arjun, and he gave her a box full of Danya's diaries. "Danya always wrote in these, even on days that nothing even happened. She filled up three to four journals a year. They're a great way for you to get to know her, to find out more about Danya. I have not gone through all of them yet, please help yourself to anything you like of hers. She would have liked that."

Dara was taken aback for a moment, but then thanked Devdas as she accepted the box, "I think that I would actually like that. Thank you."

And that was that. Six months had passed, and Dara was still there, and much more settled than she thought she ever would be. Devdas gave her a free hand with the children, and she was having a lot of fun with her daily life that she almost forgot that she really did not belong there, that it was a temporary situation. Nonetheless she was still enjoying her new life. She was going through the journals, and she found them interesting, they gave her an insight of what Danya was like as a person, and how her life with Devdas was.

'Devdas is what every man on this planet should be like. He's not perfect, nobody is, but his good qualities are such and rare that one has to wish every woman on this planet who's looking for a wonderful man to share her life with should be like, when I cried he was there to listen, to hold me and comfort me, and for me to lean on for strength. When something good happened to him, he made sure to call me and share his happiness with me—Devdas is my shelter from the world, he's like every imaginary love story's hero, but real and much, much kinder. Not once did he take me for granted, not once did I feel unsure of his love, not once did I regret marrying him... I pray that we do have more than one lifetime and I pray that I get him in each and every one of them.' Dara was saddened again by how much they missed out in not knowing each other.

Nothing can change the past, what's important is the here and now. Dara was mulling things over as she was sitting outside watching Devdas play with Arjun, and she brought out Danya's letter to read it again. 'Have you ever loved someone without actually meeting them? As strange, ridiculous and unrealistic as it sounds, that is exactly what happened to me. When I first set eyes on Devdas, I knew instantly that I loved him—some force connected me to him without words—the past four years have been a wondrous experience... an adventure, and each day my love and respect for the man I married deepens. During this pregnancy I have not been feeling my best and yet Devdas has been there for me every day no matter what, taking days off from work just to stay home and take care of me. We're not sure why I'm this tired all the time, but I have had a cold for the past two weeks, and it's not getting any better. I am just so tired of being tired! I know we have not been close growing up, not even as cousins should be, but you are the only family I have aside from Devdas, and I would love for you to come here, I would love for you to be a part of my children's lives—there is so much that we missed out on in each other's lives, but I hope that you would still have a place in your life for my family.'

The letter held new meaning to Dara now—could Danya have felt the end coming? Is that why she contacted her so urgently after all those years? She never wrote or called when she married Devdas... could she have realized that she was not going to be around much longer, and that's why she wanted Dara there? A lot of questions that Dara doubted she'd ever have the answers to. One thing she was certain of though: Danya's love for Devdas was out of this world. *How does it feel to be so in love with another human being?* It made her curious about Devdas also, to get to know him better as a person and not just because he was Danya's husband. Sitting on the wooden swing, holding Danya's letter in her lap, Dara watched as Devdas walked around the garden with Arjun, admiring the patience he showed towards the child and the love that glowed clearly on his face whenever he looked down or knelt beside his son. Dara blushed when Devdas suddenly looked up and saw her looking at him. To cover for her embarrassment she waved at them and went inside the house to put Danya's letter away.

"Dara, you have to come back outside and watch the sunset—the sky is clear and it's just magnificent, you can't miss it." She had not heard him coming in after her, and it made her blush even more. And it threw Devdas off how much alike she and Danya were in personality, even though they were never raised together! She followed him outside quietly, keeping her distance. Arjun ran to her, and she held him up in her arms. That's when she had a real smile on her face. They watched the sunset which was truly spectacular together, and then went back inside.

After dinner that evening, Devdas asked her as they were getting ready to have their after dinner chai, "Can I ask you something personal?"

Putting up her guard again, Dara squared her shoulders, and nodded a yes.

"Have you ever been engaged or married? Or is there somebody waiting for your return in Jordan?"

She answered shortly, "None. I never had relationships because I made sure never to let anybody close enough for them to be important enough to hurt me. I hurt the few that liked me before I gave them the chance. And you know what? One of them I really, really liked, he made me feel so special and so happy whenever we were together, but I followed my pattern and ran for it. Looking at my life and going through Danya's diaries, I can tell you we both were good at running away from life, we both thought it was easier than facing it. It's clear now how wrong the two of us were. I have no regrets though, I've learnt that love comes naturally, we learn to hate—it's not a good feeling, but sometimes it gets you through rough situations that love would have made you crumble through."

Devdas was shocked at her bitterness and the matter-of-fact tone, but also sensed her fear, so he tried to be more open about himself to try and make her more comfortable. "Nobody has a perfect life, and nobody can have a perfect marriage or relationship. I believe it takes two to make a marriage work, it's just not possible for one person to have the burden of holding it all together and not become resentful of the other person."

"Thank you. Unfortunately, in a lot of cases people think it's the wife's duty to hold the marriage together. No matter what happens, excuses are always made for the husband for any sort of neglect of his marriage, because the wife should take and accept anything and everything. I say it goes both ways, a person had better be willing to give as they take. I've seen a couple of my friends and an aunt give everything to their husbands, and they were all repaid with betrayal. And of course excuses were made for the men. It just drives me insane." She looked at Devdas for his reaction to her outburst, and added softly, "I finished reading Danya's last book, I can't say I was not surprised you let her write it, and let her keep her name."

Devdas laughed lightly, got up, and went around the table to help her out of her seat. Most evenings, Mrs. Khanna turned in early and they ate dinner alone.

"Danya's name was, is, her identity. She said that she did not understand why women had to change their names after marriage, like they were only somebody's daughter or sister or wife, and not human beings on their own, and I always admired her views, no matter how different they were from everybody else's. It was her wish to write and I prized her for being a strong and brave woman."

"Well, call me selfish, but I don't want to make any sacrifices in my life, it's just that simple. What is expected of women sometimes is beyond humiliating. A woman does not need to keep her integrity or dignity intact as long as she keeps her husband happy and never breaks her family home—how does anybody expect the children in such a relationship to grow into decent human beings? If they are boys, that pretty much tells them that it's okay to treat women like slaves because they will take it for they don't have much choice, and if they are girls they learn that it's fine not to have any self respect as long as the world thinks they are doing what's right by the husband and the society."

Dara stopped herself, to take in a breath and to calm herself down. She always got a little too excited, and angry, when she talked about this subject. Reading Danya's last book inflamed those feelings inside of her once more. Her father once told her that she actually got a little aggressive even. She did not mind. Her beliefs were her own strength, it did not matter if ninety percent of the world probably did not agree with her. She knew she was right.

Devdas was watching her thoughtfully and then wondered calmly, "You want to fix the world?"

Dara looked out of the window at the garden and taking another deep breath, she answered with more control. "I wish I could. Sometimes I even used to wish that God would let me rule earth for one day so I can try and change it. I know it's not God's doing that human beings are the way they are, but I still wish there was a way to erase wickedness from the world. I can't stand rude, mean and wicked people."

"Who was it who said that you can't feel happiness unless you'd seen misery first?" Devdas wondered as a way to lighten things up.

"Somebody who had nothing better to do but make up bumper stickers' slogans."

Devdas laughed, and Dara turned to look at him. She had to admit that he was a great listener, and from what she read in Danya's journals, he was a very respectful man. He had surprised her two months before with a new painting set after she told him that that was what she did for a living in Jordan. It was her passion more than her profession. She found it a very thoughtful and generous gift.

"Have you ever thought about writing a book about what you think is wrong with the world?" He was asking her now.

Taken aback for a second, Dara said laughingly, "No, thank you I'd rather not be shot to death just yet. I know most people would not agree with what I think, and I don't care to impose my beliefs on anybody." She then added more seriously, "You see, what I believe is for me alone, I could say it to everybody on this planet and write a thousand books, but nothing will ever change, it's just human nature. Not just with men and women. Some people might nod their head and agree with me, but everything will still be the same. I try to follow the serenity prayer and accept what I cannot change. I know my limitations, and I accept that I cannot change the world no matter how much I want to, and no matter how much I joke about wanting god to allow me to do it. I just try to be strong enough to survive this world."

Devdas looked at her thoughtfully, and she brought back a memory of him and Danya having a similar discussion. "I wish you and Danya had spent more time together, you have a lot of similar beliefs."

"Yeah—and that's why after everything you did she still came back to India with you...." Her jaw dropped! She always spoke her mind too honestly and more than once got in trouble for it. She looked at Devdas apprehensively, and he had a shocked, yet amused look on his face. And to her amazement it turned into a loud, heartfelt laugh.

"I'm sorry... I'm always so blunt...rude actually..." She mumbled. But still laughing, Devdas put his hand on her head, as if blessing her. She suppressed a shiver that ran down her spine. Devdas noticed, but he misunderstood her reaction, and backed away from her.

"I'm sorry, but I'm used to blessing... well, like I always told Danya I did not give her my blessings because I felt superior to her, but blessed her for the joy she brought into my life every day we were together." He breathed in heavily and went back to his seat, and took a sip of his chai. Dara stayed where she was, she'd just found out that Devdas was a very attractive man! She shook her head in bewilderment, and sat in her chair to listen to what he was saying.

"I have to agree with you, but I can't be but grateful that Danya did come back with me. And you're right about what you said. I suppose you found that in one of Danya's journals?"

She replied while looking at her nails to avoid looking into Devdas's eyes, "Yes. I've been reading them in my free time, I like to read, and you have to admit: four to five journals a year is a lot of writing!"

He smiled kindly, and somewhat sadly. "Yes, Danya could write. As for her coming back, she did it out of love, and because she believed in me more than anybody else in the world. She realized I had acted out of despair and anger, true it had been a very childish thing to do, one you could read about in a book or see in a movie and roll your eyes at. But I cannot deny that I'm happy I had married Danya, and had the chance to spend those four years with her, I wish it had been longer, but I guess we have to accept that we only had this much time to spend together, and just appreciate every moment of it. That's what death teaches you I guess, it's always better to enjoy the people you love while they're still around and you have the chance to enjoy their company, than to regret not doing that after it's too late. Danya was beautiful, loving and extremely kind. That's why I said that I wish you'd known each other more. You would have loved her, and her company."

Dara was silently evaluating Devdas. He admitted readily to wronging Danya, and from Danya, she knew that he was an extraordinary man, she was discovering this herself every day. But she was also conscious of the fact that she was becoming more aware of him as a man, not just as Danya's husband or the children's father, and it was making her extremely uncomfortable.

Devdas then brought her out of her thoughts, handing her another surprise. "You're absolutely right by the way, you know, about the fact that women are expected to shoulder the bigger sacrifices in life. I believe that one should treat people the way they want to be treated, especially when those people are kind and nice to begin with. I believe that one should never do to somebody what you don't want done to you. To always ask: what if it was the other way around?"

Dara only nodded in agreement, and had to avert her eyes. *What on earth is wrong with me? I'm becoming as sappy as every other female in this world.* She pulled herself together and said to Devdas's collarbone! She still could not look him in the eye, and her tone against her will was icy, "Danya wanted to belong, she loved you and needed you in her life for her life to feel complete. I never had that feeling about my life—I don't believe I'm incomplete as a person on my own for me to need a partner, there's nothing wrong with the way Danya felt, as there is nothing wrong with the way I feel—we are all different in this world—we just have Not really learnt to accept that or respect it about each other on this sad little planet! That bothers me the most possibly, that people do not understand that just because a person has different beliefs or different religious ideas, that does not make him or her wrong, it's just the way it is." She was staring at him now, and wondering how different he was at heart, and she involuntarily looked at his chest where the heart would be, and felt her cheeks burn. He really was a very attractive man, in personality and in looks, but then her self-preservation resurfaced. Devdas was watching her, and he could just see the change in her face, and the way she held herself together.

"I have to go check on the children now, this is why I stayed here in the first place. I'm glad we had this talk, and glad we both understand that no matter how much I would have in common with Danya, I am not her. I could never be her, and I don't want to be her."

And without stopping to look at the astounded look on Devdas's face, she went upstairs. That she spent the rest of the night crying her eyes out was for her own knowledge only.

Ten
Chori... Chori
(Slowly... Slowly)

ara woke up with the worst headache she could have ever imagined, it felt like her eyes were going to pop out of her head. She lay still for ten minutes, waiting for the pain to lessen, or hopefully go away but when it became worse to where she could not even keep her eyes open, she started to panic. *What am I going to do now? What will happen to the children if anything happens to me? Who on earth can I call?*

Before her panic attack reached its peak though, she thought she heard knocking on her door, and somebody calling out her name a couple of times, and then she definitely heard the door open, and harried footsteps stopping next to her bed.

"Are you okay? Dara? Are you all right?"

She recognized Devdas's voice, but could not even nod her head and tears started streaming down into her ears, but she could not even shake her head to clear them out. She then felt herself being moved gently and moments later she felt a cold compress on her forehead. "Don't worry, I called the doctor and he is on his way."

When the doctor finally showed up, it was to confirm that Dara had a bad case of migraines mixed with a new flu virus. Devdas insisted that she stay in her bed, and was even at her bedside every time she opened her eyes from the pain, or woke her up to take the medication. Luckily, Riya was more than capable of taking care of the children by herself, and Devdas had taken the rest of the week off from work and was helping care for Dara himself. He only left her bedside when it was time for him to go tuck the children in or go and get some sleep himself.

Zaara came two days later to visit and to check on Devdas and the children. When she was told about Dara being sick, she went up to visit and chat with her a bit. It had taken Zaara the longest to get over the shock of finding out about Dara. She could not be angry with Danya for not confiding in her, though. Nothing in the past now mattered. She smiled brightly at Dara and said softly. "I'm glad to see you looking better. Dev said that you were so pale two days ago. I think that you frightened him. He was real worried about you when I called to say that I will be visiting today. I hope you are feeling better?"

Smiling and trying not to wince at the pain that even the simplest movement still caused her, Dara replied, "Much better, thank you, and thank you for coming up to check on me."

"You're welcome, trust me it was no trouble at all, and I am glad you are well. I hope to see you soon after you're feeling better. Maybe we'll have lunch together."

And with that she left. Being with Dara unnerved her more than she could admit, and the lack of friendliness and warmth from Dara only made it harder for Zaara to be around her. Not a day goes by when she does not miss Danya. After having a cup of chai with Devdas and his mother, Zaara left, promising them she'd come back for dinner with Rohan soon. After Zaara left, Devdas went back to Dara's room to check on her and to give her a cup of herbal tea. The doctor recommended she stay away from caffeine. Devdas found her sitting up in bed with her head leaning back against the head board, eyes shut, and she was clutching Danya's letter in her hand. Devdas cleared his throat so he wouldn't startle her, and she opened those green eyes to look at him. Sometimes he could almost see a look of caring in those eyes, before the shadows ascend and then there was only coldness.

"I did not know whether you went back to sleep, but you should have something hot to drink before you do, it might soothe you more." He said as he walked to the bedside table.

Dara looked at him for a second, and then looked at her hands, reminding herself that Devdas was once Danya's husband and it would not do her any good to forget that.

"Thank you Devdas. I am feeling better now. Please, you could leave me now. You should go back to your work tomorrow. I don't want you to disrupt your life for me." As usual she was abrupt and cold.

Devdas's hand was shaking with anger, but he tried to keep his emotions under control as he set the tea cup down and then sat down in the chair next to Dara's bed. He was not going to let her shut him out like that anymore. "I am glad you are feeling better, but it is not a problem for me to take any time off from work to help you out. After all, you have taken time off from your own life and have been here for so long to help me and the children. Why won't you accept kindness when you can hand it out so easily? And don't try to ignore me as always. I want you to be honest with me for once, who hurt you like this?"

Dara winced, but looked at Devdas's face, and felt all her resolutions about never getting involved in more than taking care of the children waver. She moistened her lips and tried not to sound rude. She knew she always depended on her bluntness to alienate people, but this was one time when she could just try and be more polite in her answers. "No one." And when he looked skeptical, she added. "I told you before, I really never let anybody close enough to ever hurt me, and I was truthful when I told you that. All there is to it is that anytime I thought I had a real friend, they went and betrayed me. It happened so many times that I almost doubted myself, but then I realized it was my misfortune that I only attracted the users in the friends' department. I had no time in my life for a real relationship because I was always busy with somebody else's life. For example, one of my friends always had boy troubles and she always came to me for help, and I have that type of personality that I would get immersed in somebody else's life to where I thought of her problems as my own, and I stood by her even when she made the wrong choice for a husband. I was the only one helping her out. I have not talked to her for years, I hope he was worth it."

Dara smiled sadly at Devdas, and said, with some anger now in her voice, "I should add that that same 'friend' of mine went and betrayed me when I needed her to be there for me. You see, I had a great crush on this guy back home. I was young, sixteen, and had never had any relationship with boys, and this guy was eighteen, gorgeous, nice, kind…. If I could ever find his whereabouts I would love to tell him how special he was to me. Not love, I don't think I really loved him. I was in love with the idea of love, before I wised up that is. To make a long story short, he was a Muslim, and my so-called-friend was going to him behind my back and telling him he could do better than me, and to look for a good Muslim girl! I mean, come on, I was sixteen! It's not like I ever thought would end up marrying him! Plus there was always this guy in my life, Issam, since I was younger, I always carried some sort of love for him, but I made sure he never got close to me, and when he did try, I made his life miserable to where he ran away and never came back. You can call me childish, which I was, a coward, which I definitely was, but never stupid enough to let people hurt me again." Dara quieted down, and looking at her fingers as though embarrassed about what she'd share with him next, said, "Truthfully, Danya did try to keep in touch. That's how I knew about Fadi and Zaara. It's just that I never answered back…" And trying to keep herself composed, she added with a choked up voice he could barely hear. "I know I should have tried too, but… there are no excuses that I can think of now—it's all done with."

She closed her eyes and leaned her head back, and Devdas respected that she needed to be left to her thoughts for a minute, and tried not to judge—what would it change now? They were all gone. He looked at her intently and he could tell she was already regretting saying anything to him. He could see her closing up, but he could not do anything about it. She was making her choices and it was the least that he could do for her, to respect her wishes. When she looked into his eyes again, he knew he was right, the veil was already down. He got up, wished her good night and left.

Dara sat still in bed for five minutes, until she was sure Devdas had gone into his own room and then had to cover her face with her pillow so nobody could hear her sobbing. She felt sorry for herself, which is never a good feeling, felt sorry for Devdas and could not shake away the feeling of helplessness. She always took on somebody else's life, and now she was doing it again, but in a selfish way, she wanted this life for herself... for her, Dara, not Danya's cousin, not Danya's lookalike sister. She wanted it for herself.

Well, I know why I'm here, and they all know, I made this choice and I better be prepared not to get too attached to any of them, be prepared to leave one day when they won't need me anymore.... Come on Dara, do not get too attached—not to the children, not to maji, and definitely not to Devdas. They are not yours, and they never will be.

But while she was advising her own self about not getting attached, or too involved, it occurred to her that it was already too late for that.

It was two weeks later, through which she had been coldshouldering Devdas and trying to avoid his company as much as she possibly could. When Dara noticed in the early morning that a group of people were going on foot that day, dressed in white but sounding happy. She had learned from Mrs. Khanna that people always wore white when somebody died, so that was her first thought, that this must be a funeral procession—when people started singing and flinging colorful powder in the air and at each other. She ran downstairs and out to the gates to watch more closely. That was definitely no sad looking crowd. They were carrying a lot of that colorful powder. Some were already wearing it on their faces!

I have to show this to the kids! She ran into the children's nursery, and was shocked to find Devdas in there.

"Oh, good morning Devdas. I did not know you were up already."

"Good morning Dara. I came to wish Arjun and Zohra a good morning, and to take you all out to celebrate Holi today."

"Holi who?" She wondered as she gave each of the children a good morning hug and kiss, and edged as far away from Devdas as possible.

Devdas laughed and said, "Holi festival, it's also called the spring festival as it marks the arrival of the season of color, hope and joy. You are going to like it, trust me. Now that you all are here, I have something for you." He handed her and Arjun gift bags, and sat Zohra in his lap with hers. Dara noticed that even Riya got a gift bag in her hands. They opened them all at almost the same time. Each bag held a new colorful outfit, and both Dara and Riya got a box of sweets too. Dara held on to her gifts and raised shiny eyes to Devdas. He was smiling happily at all of them, and she smiled back.

"Thank you. This is really kind of you." And then she mumbled something about getting ready and went to her room. She held her gift closely for a second, and then checked it out. It was a traditional Indian outfit, white and simple; a long white shirt with white pants and a white wrap. It was all embroidered with fine silver thread around the edges. She got out of her clothes and put her new outfit on fast. When she looked in the mirror, she was amazed how clothes could transform a person's image.

After breakfast with Mrs. Khanna, through which she kept complimenting Dara on her new outfit, they all went out to check out the celebrations in the street. Devdas was carrying Zohra while Dara held Arjun's hand. Riya and Mrs. Khanna followed, and people started throwing paint on Dara and Arjun. She stopped in her tracks, shocked at first and even Devdas was worried about her reaction, but she burst out laughing and ran with Arjun to join the merriment. Devdas let out an amused laugh when she came back ten minutes later to where he was sitting with the rest enjoying some milk and hot jelebis at a street vendor's. She was drenched from head to toes! Water and colored powder were dripping off of her and Arjun, and she was laughing with the joy of a child. Mrs. Khanna burst out laughing at the sight of her.

"Bless you my child. Does any vendor in the market have any paint left or are you wearing it all!"

Devdas smiled kindly and said, "No, I guess she got it all."

With a huge smile, Dara grabbed a handful of the colored powder from a nearby tray and put it on Devdas's cheek. She had her hand cupping the side of his face, and just looked into his eyes for the longest moment. Shyly she lowered her gaze and hand. He almost made to grab her in a hug, but knew better than to do that in front of everybody and in the street. Add to that he was not so sure about her reaction to such a show of emotions, no matter how innocent or friendly they were. He laughed lightly and said, "I'm glad you are having a good time."

He had the feeling that she was warring with the same conflicted emotions as his. She shook her head and laughed with obvious joy, "I never knew getting so messy was so much fun! I normally get mad when I paint and get splashed with some. Do you always do this?"

"We celebrate Holi once a year in spring time. Wait till you see the bonfires and celebrations tonight. You're going to enjoy it all. You're definitely going to enjoy Diwali, the festival of lights, in November." He replied with joy at her excitement.

"Is it as much fun!" she wondered with a twinkle in her eyes.

"It is. It's as colorful and with great food, not as messy, but the lights and fireworks are dazzling. You are going to hear firecrackers at the crack of dawn so be prepared for that."

They split the rest of the day playing with colors and enjoying all the festivities. By the time they made it home at night both children were already asleep. After tucking them in bed, Dara excused herself and went to wash off and turn in for the night.

She laughed at her own reflection—she was unrecognizable from all the colors. And then she looked at her right hand and remembered holding Devdas's face. She stood there fighting with her increasing attraction to him. And then looked again at her tear streaked face in the mirror. *You are losing your grip on reality and your mind Dara. He is NOT yours.*

She could not sleep well, thoughts and worries just kept

waking her up all night. She tried warm milk and a long hot shower. Nothing would soothe her. She stood under the hot water and cried until she had no tears left. She had spent her life running away from heartache, and it came to her with vengeance!

At dawn she made her way down to the temple and prayed. To her all the religious differences did not matter at that point. Faith and believing in goodness of heart does not have an assigned name or religion.

Days were going by smoothly, or as smooth as could be expected. Dara tried hard to distance herself from Devdas, and kept herself busy caring for the children and Mrs. Khanna. When Diwali came, she did not join in the festivities, but stayed at the house by herself. Devdas did not comment on her choices of distancing herself from his culture, and accepted it for whatever it was.

Eleven
Second chance at life

"Why are you always so full of anger? Every time I try to talk to you about everyday matters, you turn it into an argument. I would like to talk to you about the weather without fearing it might turn into a war of words Dara."

Dara turned towards him again, she had just sent Arjun and Zohra to play outside, and Devdas had made the suggestion that they could hire someone to come and help with the children, so she could have more free time to do something for herself. Riya had left them after she got married and moved to Agra. Dara had turned on him angrily. "I have been doing just fine for the last two and a half years Devdas, and I think I can manage until Zohra goes to school also."

After she made sure the children were within view, she replied to his argument, "I'm not angry. I told you I am okay with taking care of the children by myself and ma*ji* helps also. As for not talking about anything else, I've already told you I don't care to discuss anything about my life, I've already told you enough. You really need to understand this once and for all Devdas: I am not Danya, I did not really know Danya, and I'm not like her, I don't want to change the world, I don't have it in me, and I don't want to even try. I really just want the world to leave me alone. What matters is what I do now and here, and how I take care of the children. "

And she turned and followed the children outside. Devdas could not understand how such a simple comment could turn into such an argument. He knew Danya and Dara were two different people, and could understand why Dara would be this sensitive about it, especially after what happened on that night long ago when he mistook her for Danya, but really that had been so long ago, and he never ever brings up Danya with her anymore. She did—a lot! It was as if she was using Danya as a shield between them. He still felt like she was pushing him away every time he tried to be friendly or show her some appreciation for staying and helping with the children. She did put her life on hold while he was trying to sort out his. If he was to be honest, he did not even think that her and Danya looked that much alike even, not anymore, for Dara to keep suggesting that he keeps treating her as if she was Danya.

Frustrated with her attitude, Devdas decided for the hundredth time not to ever bother and try and understand Dara anymore. It was Zaara who brought it up. She came over to visit, and check on Devdas and the children. After Dara said hello, she took Zaara's little boy, Aditya, to play outside with Arjun and Zohra, leaving Devdas and Zaara to have tea. "I like her Dev. I know we did not strike a great friendship, me and her, but I still like her. She's so reserved, I have a feeling she's afraid of facing the world and reality, and that's why she's always on the defensive. She attacks before giving anybody the chance to hurt her."

"I see that sometimes, but, I don't know—sometimes we would be having just a normal conversation and she turns it into an argument, always alluding that I do not know enough to tell the difference, like I can't tell who she really is... she drives me insane."

Zaara laughed, and pointed out. "You two actually sound like an old married couple. You have to admit that you enjoy the debates."

Sighing deeply, Devdas put his cup down, and looked outside, watching Dara playing with the children, that was the only time she truly looked happy and carefree, he could hear her laughter. "I just miss talking to another person, another adult, aside from ma*ji*, and people from work. You know what I mean?"

Smiling kindly at Devdas, Zaara said gently. "I know, I understand the difference. You were used to having Danya to talk to, and she was a great talker, and it's been different. I'm sorry I don't come around more. You know how it is."

"I know, and I understand. Rohan is being too good natured about this, but I would never want to cause you and him any problems."

"He's really been great about everything. For now, let's worry about you while I'm here—I know it's hard for you to consider this now, but you need a companion in your life. Danya would want you to move ahead with your life, for you, for ma*ji*, and for the children. Just try and think about it."

It was weeks later, when Mrs. Khanna brought him the news that one of their well-known family friends had sent feelers for a marriage proposal. For the first time, Devdas said yes without stopping to think. Her name was Kaaya Rampal. Her father was a good friend of Devdas's father, and had stayed in touch with the Khanna family over the years even after they, the Rampal's, had moved to Australia and started their own successful business there. When Mrs. Khanna sent them Devdas's approval, they decided to travel to India within a month to set things going, but Kaaya was to arrive within a week, to give her and Devdas a chance to get to know each other for a while before things were really decided.

Since Dara had insisted on being a private person, Mrs. Khanna thought that Devdas had told her about his coming marriage, and Devdas thought the same of his mother.

Kaaya was to stay with her aunt close by, and they stopped by the Khanna household for tea on the second day of her arrival. Dara came downstairs, holding Zohra in her arms, and exchanged some pleasantries with Kaaya and her aunt. It wasn't until they all sat outside in the garden, that Kaaya's aunt, Roopa, mentioned the coming engagement party. Dara nearly choked on her tea. She was looking at Devdas and Kaaya, and felt her chest tighten—if hearts could break, hers was chattered into a billion pieces—and she realized with horror that she loved Devdas! No... she was in love with Devdas!!!

Dara excused herself hastily, and almost ran inside. *How could I love Devdas?* And a small voice in her head answered: *How could I not? I have to get out of here... maybe it is time I went back home.* And she realized with a pang that she had been considering India her home for the past two and a half years. Never in a million years would she have imagined to be so desperately in love, and to top it off, with Danya's husband. Could Danya have foreseen all of this happening? Did she love her husband so much, she was willing to have her substitute ready on hand? Obviously her plans never calculated for Devdas marrying somebody else. Dara was so used to her life in the Khanna household that she almost forgot that she never intended to stay this long in the first place.

Kaaya was very nice, and very beautiful. She loved the children, and even they had warmed up to her faster and easier than Dara would have imagined. *What else could anybody want? And didn't somebody once say that if you loved someone you'd want them to be happy, even if their happiness was not with you?*

"I would love to meet the genius who said that and give him a good kick." She was mumbling to herself, and did not notice Kaaya coming towards her until the latter spoke. "You have done wonders with the children, and the garden. Devdas showed me where you started the flower garden, it's beautiful."

Her words were so sincere that Dara could not but like her also, and answered truthfully. "Thank you. They are wonderful children. I am going to miss them very much." Tearing up, she averted her gaze. Not only was she losing Devdas, she was also losing her children. To her Zohra and Arjun were hers now. They even had taken to calling her Dara*ma* without any of the adults ever paying attention to it, but now it all came rushing to Dara as she was about to lose it all.

"Devdas said you used to live in Jordan, but have been

here for almost three years. Have you considered moving to India for good to be close to the children?"

Taken aback, Dara answered her, "To tell you the truth, it had just dawned on me that I did not come here to stay. I still don't know what I'm going to do."

"I honestly would hate to see you leave us, please don't take our getting married as a way for us to try and deprive you of the children. I would never do that to you or to them."

Dara held Kaaya's hand for a second and with a choked voice thanked her, before excusing herself and going back inside the house to hide in her room until her tears dried up... again.

Devdas asked her to join him in his office that evening. She arrived feeling restless, uncomfortable, and nervous. Since she had realized her true feelings for him, she had been avoiding his presence, and when they did meet she did not dare look into his face, a face that she had come to love so much, she now understood what Danya was saying when she once wrote that she was addicted to looking at Devdas's beautiful dimples.

That's another thing I would have had in common with Danya: being pathetic when we love this man.

When she got to his office, she took a steadying breath, knocked on the door and went inside. He was standing next to his desk, and she just stared at him. How could she not have realized before that her animosity towards him was all the work of her self-preservation? That it was actually covering up for her increasing love and attraction towards him? Clearing a lump in her throat and shaking her head to clear her thoughts, she said. "You wanted to see me Devdas?"

"Yes, please sit down." He waited until she was seated before handing her a glass of juice, and sitting down with one of his own. *Great, as if I needed more proof that he is wonderfully lovable.* She was thinking to herself. To him she said.

"Thank you, Devdas."

"Kaaya told me she talked to you about what your plans for the future are and I wanted to make sure you understand that my marriage changes nothing, you are welcome to stay here for as long as you wish. And as you can tell the children are not going to give you up easily." Smiling his gorgeous sideway smile and showing her the dimples she'd come to love, he added a little awkwardly, if possible for a man his age to be made uncomfortable by anything. "To be honest with you, I don't think I want to even think about you leaving us."

That deepened the color in her face and she mumbled with a breathless voice. "Thank you. I would love to stay here. I might have to go to Jordan to take care of my affairs over there, and visit with my friends, and then I will come back after you and Kaaya had settled down with the children a bit. I'm going to arrange my ticket for next week at most. I will try and be back within three months, and when I do, I will arrange to move out into my own place."

And please, oh God, please do not ask me to be here and watch you get married.

Devdas almost lost his self-control... *how cold can she be?* But he was calm when he said. "Do as you please, Dara. And as for moving out, please accept my offer for you to move into the guest house, consider it yours as of now. This way you can have your own place and still be close to us... I mean, close to the children."

She was so close to tears now, her vision so blurry that she could barely see his face, so she took a sip of her juice, and excused herself hastily, "If that would be all Devdas, good night then. And thanks for the offer. I'll let you know soon." And she almost ran out of his office.

Now I know what me and Danya would have had in common the most, we both want to hold Devdas and keep him safe and happy, no matter what it would have done to our sanity.

She went straight to her room, and actually started throwing her clothes inside her suitcase... she had to leave soon. *What a pathetic person I turned out to be... I will leave and I know my heart and soul are attached to the people residing in this house until the end of time....... Oh God, please, please help me.*

Devdas stayed in his office thinking things over. He could not believe that she could be this unaffected by his marriage. He had expected some sort of reaction if he was to be honest with himself, but got none. Well, except that she looked sad about leaving the children for a while. *What did I expect? That all of a sudden she'd look at me as more than Danya's husband or the children's father? Nice try.*

The next day, Devdas took Kaaya out to a late lunch. He was beginning to like her, who wouldn't, and again it was Kaaya who brought up Dara. "I hope she does not take it personal or the wrong way and think I want to take her place in the house. She is very nice, and the children love her, it would be great if she'd stay." And her beautiful light brown eyes sparkled with a sudden thought, "Dev, what do you think of introducing Dara to my brother Rahul? It would be great if they got to like each other and maybe got married.

He's about to open a branch for my father's company here, so she would always be close to the children."

It was Devdas's turn to nearly choke on his food, he had to take a sip of his drink and cough a couple of times before he was able to answer. "Are you serious? Why?"

"What do you mean why? Dara is a really nice person, pretty and smart, and my brother is good looking, responsible, kind and smart also, so why not?"

Wiping his mouth with his napkin, and placing it next to his plate, he looked at Kaaya, and noticed for the first time that she was a really beautiful woman. He tried to answer truthfully, to an extent.

"If Dara was more accepting of our culture like Danya was, I would have said go for it. I would not have believed it, for two people to look so much alike, and yet be so very different. Danya was a warm and loving person—Dara can be very cold and practical. Don't get me wrong, she's nice, but the only times I see her at ease are when she is with the children. She has been living with us for so long and not once had she acted carefree, and whenever she did, she'd turn around and shut me out for days and weeks. I don't know if your brother would even be happy with somebody who's not comfortable with our culture and who is so independent. She makes it very clear she needs nobody in her life."

Kaaya laughed and patted his hand. "If I didn't know any better, I would have thought that you don't want Dara to get married and leave you."

"What?" Devdas mumbled. A 'what' that made Kaaya look at him thoughtfully. But before jumping to her own conclusions, she added softly, "Dev, I think you're acting a bit selfish here. I realize you've definitely gotten used to having

Dara help out with the children, and maybe the household, but it's not a kind thing to stop her from having her own life, or her own children. She's what, Thirty- something? This is her time to have a life and a family of her own."

Looking genuinely surprised and annoyed at being called selfish... and the idea of Dara moving away! Worse—getting married! "This is not it. I can't believe you'd even suggest this is what my motive is. I have not gotten used to having her here, because...."

Moving his hand away from Kaaya's, and holding his head in his hands, he added, "Because as weird as it sounds, it feels like she has always been here—and it's not a sick thing where I think she is Danya, or to be as delusional in thinking that Danya did not die. I can tell this is Dara, but the way she'd settled into our lives, even though you can tell she does not even like it as much here, she's at ease mostly, like she always belonged here. I know it doesn't make a lot of sense. But this is the truth of it."

He leaned back in his seat, still avoiding looking into Kaaya's face, and even though he noticed her silence, he continued. "She is so independent to the point of it being rude and irritating—she does the gardening, her own laundry, and sometimes the children's. She cooks for herself because she prefers Middle Eastern food, and won't accept anybody's help unless she's really stuck on something and has to accept help. To be honest I don't know what the kids are going to do when she leaves—even my mother is so attached to her." Devdas exhaled slowly, and looked at Kaaya with one of the saddest expressions she'd ever seen.

"Maybe you are somewhat right, I had gotten used to her being there for my family that I forgot that she might not want to stay for always." He laughed a bit ruefully, "You know, she has never watched a Hindi movie? She mostly prefers to read, and only suspense/horror books, she actually said that romance novels bore her that is why she only read one of Danya's books, the last one which had nothing to do with romance."

Kaaya was not even smiling now, but she was feeling some newfound knowledge blossom in her mind. Devdas noticed her expression, and misunderstood it.

"I'm sorry. I have to be the worst type of husband-to-be there is, I have been talking to you out of all people about Danya and Dara and we have not talked about you once since we got here. I'm really sorry."

Kaaya held her drink, and sat back in her seat, watching Devdas carefully. They talked about the differences of life in India and Australia, his work, her work, but not once about their future. When they got back to the Khanna house, Kaaya was going to stop there for chai before Devdas was to drive her home, they heard laughter coming from the flower garden and they walked towards it. Dara was sitting on the ground, with mud all over her face, and Arjun just laughing as if it was the funniest thing he'd ever seen. He had thrown the mud at her, and was admiring his work. Dara got up, laughing, and then she picked up the little boy, and held him tightly to her. Devdas said nothing, but felt a tightening in his chest so he turned and went inside the house. Kaaya watched Dara and Arjun for another minute, and then followed Devdas inside.

They did not talk about Dara or Rahul again, but when Devdas dropped her off later on, Kaaya turned to him in the car and said before getting out.

"Dev, I really like you, and it would be ridiculous of me

to say that marrying you is not something that would make me and my family happy. But I want to be honest with myself also. I think you have deeper feelings for Dara than you even know, and it would do us all well if you figured things out before we go anywhere from here." And smiling a good night, she got out of the car without waiting for a response, figuring she'd have to wait a while for the stunned look on Devdas's face to subside and for him to find his voice again. It actually took Devdas five whole minutes to shake himself out of the shock and drive away.

The next morning, Zaara and Rohan stopped by for tea and Devdas complained to Zaara about Kaaya accusing him of having feelings for Dara. He was almost outraged.

"Really! Why would I have feelings for someone who keeps fighting and arguing with me nonstop? Am I grateful to her for all she's done for us? Of course I am, but nothing of what Kaaya was alluding to. It's out of question. I can't."

Zaara laughed, and said knowingly. "You know what I think? Kaaya is smarter than you and I put together. How did I not notice? You enjoy these debates that you two get into more than anything, and I only see you looking so alive after you and her had slugged it out for a little bit. I haven't seen you this way since Danya first left you and went back to the states. I like Kaaya, but I think she is right, and if you have feelings for Dara you should deal with that first. Find out where you two stand before going forward with any of your wedding plans. That would be the right thing to do by everybody involved."

Rohan nodded in agreement as Zaara tilted her head, laughed lightly and said, "You need to watch out though, Dara is a bigger dreamer than Danya ever was, and the funny thing is that she does not even realize it herself. She tries to keep up this tough guy image around her to guard herself from the world."

After Zaara and Rohan left, Devdas went for a long walk to clear his thoughts, and then with a heavy heart went to talk to his mother. She was sitting in the living room watching a serial on the television, but she turned it off when she saw the look on Devdas's face. He said quickly with a broken voice, "I decided to let Dara go back to Jordan by next week. I hope you're going to be okay with it."

His mother looked stricken, and asked him, "What happened? Did she say she wants to leave?"

Looking tired and unsure for the first time since Dara came to India, Devdas answered his mother truthfully. "I cannot marry Kaaya either. I already called her and told her I will be meeting with her tomorrow so we could clarify things between us, and also to extend my apologies to her parents."

"But what happened? I thought you were all set about this marriage."

"Honestly ma, I think—I know, I will never be a good husband to Kaaya, or anybody else for that matter, because... because I am in love with Dara." It was a relief and torture to finally admit to the truth.

His mother looked at him with a mixture of sadness and surprise. "I wish I had known this, I would have told you that she is my first choice for a wife for you."

When Devdas had the same look of surprise on his face, his mother chuckled and said, "How was anybody to know that you loved her for herself, and not because she's a copy of Danya, Or even because she's Danya's sister? I would love to have her as a daughter-in-law. She already is like a daughter to me."

"I can't do this to her ma*ji*. I have to let her go. I love Dara, for herself, not for Danya or because of Danya. But I want Dara to be sure of my love for her, and she never would. I don't want her to doubt for one second that I see *her* when I look into her face, that I hear her voice when she talks to me. Anytime I said something nice to her, or even if I looked at her, she always stopped to say that she's Dara and not Danya, as if to remind me in case I was ever confused. This is why I want her to go. I could never stand to see the look of fear she gets in her eyes whenever I look at her. At first I thought if she could live nearby, I'd get over it and move on with my life with Kaaya, but I'd almost went crazy when Kaaya was trying to get Dara to meet and maybe marry her brother Rahul—and Kaaya found out how I truly feel about Dara before I even did. This is why I want Dara to go back to Jordan. I have been so selfish I almost forgot that she had a life of her own before she came here, and that she did not even come to stay. She had so selflessly left her life behind to take care of my children and our household, and not once complained. But it's time I let go of my selfishness and give her back the freedom to leave. I have to let her go ma."

"No... you don't."

It was Dara who'd spoken. She walked in from the garden, with tears rolling down her face, but she had the most brilliant smile also. Devdas stood up, and looked a bit hesitant as to what to do or say—but it was Dara who took matters into her own hands. She walked up to him and clung onto him, now sobbing. Mrs. Khanna was crying too, but smiling. Devdas was standing there, patting Dara on the back and somewhat hurt that his mother could smile at a time like this instead of checking on Dara, but then she seemed to understand something that he did not.

Dara pulled back from him, but just enough to look up into his face, she kept her hold on him as if she would never let go. And she was looking up at him with the happiest face he'd seen in a very long time. "You don't have to send me anywhere, Devdas. I will never leave you. Never. I, uh....."

And finally it clicked in his heart and mind, and he held onto her this time. "I love you Dara. I love you, and only you, very much, I think I have fallen in love with you for so long that I never even realized it myself—I had to almost lose you to realize it. I love you for the kind, wonderful and giving person that you are, and I would be the happiest man on this planet if you agreed to stay here and marry me."

"I do... I love you Devdas, more than I'd ever imagined I could love anybody in my entire life. I want nothing more than to share the rest of my life with you, and your family." And not minding that his mother was still watching them with a happy and thankful smile on her face, Devdas bent his head down, and kissed his beloved, Dara...... and prayed and thanked the heavens for giving him a second chance at life, and love.

A new beginning

Writer's note:

I almost went for an alternate ending where Devdas ends up marrying Kaaya, and Dara moved back to Jordan permanently, which would have been closer to reality, but then I realized this has nothing to do with reality: it's about escaping it and hopefully having that warm feeling of love and hope in our hearts. I still hope I did not disappoint, and I still hope to have put a smile on the reader's face. All my best wishes for a happy beginning AND ending.

Preview of the upcoming book by R.K. Shadid, co-written by N.S. Karadsheh.

As Tami and her cousin Diala turned around the corner, she noticed the shop with the familiar name on the sign. "Oh, dear Lord! That is not possible! Diala, do you remember Omar? That's his family name—it must be a relative of his. Last I heard, he'd moved to Canada… you know, after all that had happened between us. I wonder if we could go in there and ask…." And she stopped in her tracks. Right there in front of her eyes, a man stepped out of the store, a man she could not forget no matter how long it had been since she'd set eyes on him last, or how far she had traveled. He looked up, almost turned around, and did a double take. "Tami?!? That's not possible!"